Love's SECRET IDENTITY

Rachel J. Good

Annie's®

AnniesFiction.com

Library of Congress-in-Publication Data
Love's Secret Identity / by Rachel J. Good
p. cm.
I. Title
                            2017963684

AnniesFiction.com
(800) 282-6643
Hearts of Amish Country™
Series Creator: Shari Lohner
Series Editor: Jane Haertel

10 11 12 13 14 | Printed in China | 9 8 7 6 5 4 3 2 1

1

Katie Kurtz inhaled a breath of crisp autumn air as she opened the mailbox. No telling what she'd find inside. She pulled out her father's weekly *Die Botschaft* Amish newspaper, a circle letter from her cousin, and—

Her hand trembled as she lifted the final envelope and shut the metal box. Dread pooled in her stomach.

Although the letter from the bank was addressed to her *Daed*, Katie tore it open. She'd taken over the responsibility for paying bills while he was recovering. Pulling out the notice, Katie unfolded and read it. Her fingers began to shake. She had feared this. The bank was foreclosing on their house.

Last month, they'd received a notice they owed a huge amount of back property taxes, and they were in danger of losing the house. Now this. As hard as she and her younger brothers and sisters worked, they'd never be able to pay these debts. Daed had only recently started to overcome his depression following *Mamm's* death two years ago, and the bills had piled up until Katie took over. He'd started working again, but he struggled to find masonry jobs.

Katie trudged into the house and sank onto the bench at the scarred maple table. Usually the aroma of chicken corn soup with its tang of onions and steamy broth made the kitchen feel homey and comforting, but its warmth couldn't penetrate the chill in her chest.

Bowing her head, Katie whispered a prayer, *Please, Lord, show me what to do about these bills.*

The front door banged open and her youngest sister, Lizzie, burst into the house, yelling, "Katie! Katie, where are you?"

At fourteen, Lizzie should be more ladylike, but without a mother to discipline her, all the training fell to Katie.

"Calm down, Lizzie," Katie called, but with little hope of quieting her sister's exuberance. She slid the foreclosure notice under the newspaper. This was another worry she'd keep to herself.

Flushed and out of breath, Lizzie galloped into the kitchen. As usual, her *Kapp* was slightly askew, the front of her apron was spotted, and tendrils of hair had escaped from the loose rolls on the side of her head. "There you are. Katie, you have to come to the market tomorrow because—" She talked so fast her words blended together.

"Take a breath," Katie said. "The news will keep."

"Not this news." Lizzie drew in a breath. "Today, this lady—"

Sixteen-year-old Leah entered the kitchen. Katie smiled at the contrast between her sisters. Leah was delicate and fair, the opposite of Lizzie's big-boned build and thick, dark hair. With Katie's red hair and petite frame, strangers often questioned if the three of them were really sisters. Her sisters worked at the Pennsylvania Dutch Farmers Market in Cockeysville, Maryland—Leah at a craft stall and Lizzie at a meat stall that sold barbecued chicken and ribs, which explained her splattered apron. That, and her youngest sister's tendency to rush into things.

Leah walked over to the table, opened the fat zippered pouch in her hands, and dumped bills and coins on the table. "We did well today. And I assume Lizzie told you about the soaps."

"Not yet, but why don't you wait and tell everyone at dinner? The goats need to be milked now." After her sisters went to the barn, Katie counted the money. They'd made enough to pay one of the smaller bills. She slid the foreclosure notice from under the newspaper and carried it upstairs to her dresser. Opening the top drawer made her stomach clench. The pile of bills and notices kept growing, and she placed the latest one on the towering stack. She set the money beside it, giving herself a little hope.

Pasting a smile on her face, she hurried downstairs to help with milking their four goats. Her sisters always saved Buttermilk for her because she was the only one who could control the mischievous doe.

As she crossed the yard, Lizzie shouted, "Buttermilk!"

Katie yanked open the barn door to help, and Buttermilk came charging through. Katie whirled and sprinted after the goat. The lively goat loved to eat the grass beside the road, but she sometimes pranced out into the street. Most drivers skidded to a stop when they spotted her, but someday . . . Katie couldn't bring herself to think about what could happen.

Katie raced faster and snagged the goat's collar just before she trotted into traffic. She held Buttermilk far away from her so the doe wouldn't nip at her skirt and apron. They made it to the barn before Buttermilk tried twisting away. Tightening her grip, Katie led the goat onto the milking platform and secured her head in place so she couldn't get away.

Leah was already milking Cinnamon, so she handed Katie the wipes for Buttermilk. Despite the doe's twitching and bucking, Katie managed to clean her. Then she set the pail under her, hoping the goat wouldn't kick it over the way she sometimes did. For once, Buttermilk stayed fairly calm and only kicked the pail once. With a quick grab, Katie saved it from tipping.

With all four goats milked, they headed in for dinner. Daed and their two younger brothers were washing up. Katie set the bowls of chicken corn soup on the table while Leah sliced one of the loaves of bread Katie had made earlier in the day. The others were lined up on the counter, ready for the farmers market in the morning.

Lizzie filled milk glasses and thumped one onto the table. At Daed's pained expression, she slowed down and set his carefully in front of him. Daed nodded his approval, and Lizzie beamed. She tried harder with the next one, but was so busy watching Daed that she sloshed milk over her hand and onto the table. Katie handed her a towel to clean up the spill, then slid into her place at the table.

After Lizzie sat down, they all bowed their heads for prayer. They repeated the Lord's Prayer silently as they always did, and then Katie added a brief request for help with finances.

When she lifted her head, the others had all picked up their spoons. No one spoke as they ate their first few mouthfuls, but then Lizzie spoke to Daed.

"This Englisher came to the stand today and bought all of Katie's soaps. She wants Katie to come with us tomorrow." Once again, Lizzie's rapid-fire words could barely be understood. "I hope she wants to buy more things."

"I'm glad you had good sales." Daed lifted his spoon to his lips, but stopped. "And you explained why Katie couldn't come?"

He directed his question to Lizzie, but it was Leah who answered. "I'm sorry, Daed." She seemed close to tears. "I told her Katie would be there."

Katie hurried to Leah's rescue. "If this English lady is expecting me, I should go."

Daed frowned. "Is that wise? A whole day at the market when you could be here working?"

Katie sighed inwardly. She usually stayed home to catch up on chores, make more crafts and baked goods to sell, and fix meals. Taking a day off tomorrow to travel to the market meant fewer items to sell next week. The bank letter made skipping a day of work even more dire, but if her sister had already promised, Katie couldn't make a liar out of her.

Leah bit her lip. "I shouldn't have told her you'd come."

"It's all right." Katie didn't want to make Leah feel guiltier than she already did. "I can take some work with me or offer to help at another stand." She gave Leah a reassuring smile. "We'll work it out." Although Katie had no idea how.

The next morning they rose at four to dress, eat breakfast, and milk the goats before the van arrived. After she and her sisters had loaded their baked goods and crafts into the back, Katie squeezed in next to one of the Stauffer sisters. The van was packed with the usual sellers, who all greeted her with surprise. She settled into her seat and set the wicker basket containing her craft supplies on her lap. She planned to get as much work done as she could while she was gone.

During the long ride on twisting back roads, Katie dozed off several times, but tried to participate in the lively conversations swirling around her whenever she woke. They reached the market at dawn, and everyone helped unload the goods. Katie pulled her black sweater close to ward off the chill, picked up an armload of containers, and carried them into the market before returning for more. Around her, people chattered as they uncovered cases, set up displays, and made multiple trips out to the hired vans.

After she'd helped Leah arrange the tables, Katie headed to the pretzel stand. She couldn't resist the smell. She bought a few pretzels that she shared with her sisters and other stand workers, then she settled onto a chair in the corner and set to work quilting a small pillow top.

Once the market doors opened to the public, the aisles were filled with customers. Several times Katie laid aside her project to assist Leah and Becka, the stand owner, in helping customers. The day passed with no sign of the Englisher.

As they were packing to leave, Leah turned to her with teary eyes. "I'm so sorry I made you come today. I thought—"

Katie placed a hand on her sister's arm. "It's all right. You couldn't have known." The day hadn't been totally wasted. She'd finished the pillow top and cross-stitched designs on several tea towels. "Besides, it was nice for me to have a chance to talk with so many people. It gets lonely at home sometimes with everyone gone."

Her sister raised an eyebrow, clearly unconvinced, but she nodded and lifted the last empty container into the back of the van.

"Yoo-hoo!" A blonde in a cream-colored cardigan set and tan pants hurried toward them.

Leah grabbed Katie's arm. "That's her. The lady I told you about."

The woman approached Leah, heels tapping across the ground. "I'm so sorry I'm late. I got caught in traffic. Is your sister here?"

When Leah introduced Katie, the blonde stared from one to the other. "You don't look much alike."

Katie smiled. "That's what everyone says. Is there something I can help you with?" She hated keeping the van waiting, but she'd come all this way to talk to this woman.

"Yes, I hope so." The woman's toothy smile belonged on one of those advertising signs along the road. "You make the goat milk soap?" When Katie nodded, she smiled. "I'm Monique Dubois."

"Pleased to meet you." Katie shook the Englisher's hand. "I'm Katie Kurtz."

"I know." Monique studied Katie for a few seconds. "I've heard good things about you from the other stand owners I work with, and the market owner vouched for you. I hope you don't mind that I checked you out first, but I need to be cautious in my business dealings."

Katie tried not to squirm under her scrutiny. "I see." It seemed a lot of trouble for buying several dozen bars of soap, but some Englishers were overly suspicious. Katie had worked at the market for years before Mamm died.

Monique opened her huge, leather purse and pulled out a stack of papers. "I own a chain of spas and would like to sell your soaps there. Would you be able to make enough to cover these orders?" She held out several sheets of paper with spa locations and numbers beside each.

Katie stared at the list. Many of the spas had requested hundreds. "I-I guess so." She had no idea how she'd make that many soaps, but she'd do whatever it took. "When would you need them?"

"In the next few weeks? Would that work?"

Katie's heart sank. "Goat milk soaps take four weeks to cure. To make that many bars would take several months."

The woman frowned. "Would it be possible to have them before Black Friday? I think they'd make wonderful Christmas gifts."

"Black Friday?"

"The day after Thanksgiving."

Katie smiled to herself. She'd only been trying to calculate the soap curing dates, but the Englisher assumed she didn't understand. Amish stores had good sales on that day when the English world went into a buying frenzy. "We could make that deadline." As long as she could get enough milk from nearby goat farmers.

Monique beamed. "Wonderful. Now with a bulk order like this, I'd expect to get the soaps for half price."

Hoping she wouldn't lose the sale, Katie said, "I barely mark up my soap, and for such a large order, I'd need to buy more molds and equipment."

Monique's eyebrows rose, then she pursed her lips thoughtfully. "Suppose I pay for those? I can get them at a dealer discount. That would save us both money."

"The supplies would help quite a bit, but could we raise the price per bar a little?"

Monique tapped her finger against her lip, making Katie nervous. As she was about to agree to the Englisher's price, Monique named a figure that was slightly lower than Katie wanted. But it would take years of farmer's market sales to make the amount Monique would pay her in a few months, so Katie agreed.

The Englisher reached into her purse again. "The other Amish I work for won't sign contracts, but if you could verify this form with your contact information, I'd appreciate it." Monique jotted the price per bar at the top. "And also list the supplies you'll need under the price."

She must have gotten Katie's contact information from the market owner's records because everything was correct, even the phone number of their English neighbor. After perusing the paper, Katie added the information Monique had requested.

When Katie handed back the paper, Monique held out perfectly manicured fingers. "Shall we shake on it?"

Delighted, Katie shook her hand. How quickly God had answered her prayers.

Then Monique dug in her purse and pulled out a small stack of bills. "Most of my suppliers at the market prefer to be paid in cash, so here's a deposit to purchase ingredients. I'll pay in full when I receive each delivery. Oh, and I'll have the molds and equipment delivered to your sister's stand early next week."

Stunned, Katie took the money.

"I look forward to doing business with you, Katie Kurtz. I'll stop by in four weeks or so to pick up the first batch. My contact information is on the order sheet if you need to reach me for any reason."

"Thank you for the order," Katie said, but Monique was already gliding away, her movements smooth and polished.

Still dazed, Katie climbed into the van and thanked everyone for waiting. She was quiet on the way home, engrossed in tallying up the orders and calculating the amount of supplies—and time—the order would take. If everyone in the family helped, she should be able to do it, but first she'd need to find a milk supplier. Their four goats produced only enough milk for the family, with enough left over for a few bars of soap.

If her figuring was correct, though, she'd make enough money to pay the taxes and most of the mortgage payments. With the money Daed and her sisters brought in, it might cover everything. Their church would donate funds to help, but Daed was adamant about not letting anyone know about their financial situation. Katie bowed her head and murmured a prayer of gratitude.

Now her only problem was getting a large enough milk supply. They couldn't afford to buy that many goats or house and feed such a large herd. She'd need to depend on one of the nearby farms.

After making the rounds of all the milk suppliers she could think of the next day, Katie wondered if this was a blessing after all. Not one of the goat farmers had agreed to supply the milk. They all claimed to be committed to Ray Gifford, an English distributor. Even when Katie offered to pay more than Ray, the farmers refused.

She had one more goat farm to try, but she held out little hope. It was smaller than the others and owned by Mose Hertzler's youngest son, Elam. Katie was friendly with Elam's cousin Miriam, so she'd spent time with him occasionally when they were younger. To Katie's disappointment, Elam rarely socialized with the others. Instead, he was a quiet loner who always had a book in his hands. Her cheeks heated as she recalled talking loudly and showing off to attract his attention when she was twelve and thirteen. He'd only frowned in her direction and gone back to reading.

Katie didn't imagine he'd make much of a goat farmer, but she was desperate, so she shook off her embarrassment and steered the buggy toward the Hertzler farm.

No one came out to meet her when she pulled in the driveway, so Katie hesitated, torn between knocking at the back door and entering the barn. She chose the barn, but found it empty. The goats were outside in the pasture, but a strange clicking noise came from the closed door of the small office inside the barn. Katie headed over and knocked.

"I'll be right out," a voice growled.

Katie stepped back a few feet. The man hadn't sounded friendly or welcoming. She hoped she hadn't interrupted something important.

The clicking continued for a few more minutes before he emerged. His brow furrowed when he spied her. He studied her for a few minutes, stroked his chin, and said, "Katie, isn't it?" When she nodded, he continued, "You're Miriam's young friend."

Young friend made her sound like she was a toddler. Katie bristled, but then let go of her irritation. No point in antagonizing someone she was about to ask for a favor. Besides, she should be loving and accepting of everyone—even goat farmers who made her feel immature and incompetent. Shaking off her negative thoughts, Katie explained why she'd come.

Before she even finished her first sentence, Elam shook his head. "Sorry, but I'm already committed to someone else."

"Ray Gifford?" she asked bitterly.

"Yes." The sharpness of Elam's answer made her feel as if she were prying.

Holding back the tears threatening to spill over, Katie asked one last question. "Would you consider switching if I paid you more money?" She tried not to sound desperate, even though he was her last hope.

Head tilted to one side, Elam stared at her. Katie couldn't tell if he was considering her offer or evaluating her. Finally, he spoke. "I don't think so."

"But my family—" Katie burst out, then pinched her lips shut.

Elam had been turning to go, but he stopped and pinned her with that stare again. "What about your family?"

"Never mind," Katie said.

"You started to say something," Elam insisted.

"It doesn't matter." Katie squirmed under his intense gaze.

"Words always matter. And I dislike unfinished sentences."

"I have a huge order for goat milk soap, and my family needs the money, but nobody will sell me milk to make it." *Satisfied?* she wanted to ask him.

He seemed to be expecting her to say more, not that it was any of his business. Katie wanted to wipe that questioning look from his face.

"If I don't make the soaps, we'll probably lose our farm."

"Probably?"

"Definitely," Katie snapped and whirled to go.

She was almost to the barn door when he spoke. "No one should lose their home. I'll sell you the milk, but only if you agree to certain conditions."

Katie didn't know what he'd expect, but he'd offered the first glimmer of hope. She'd consider doing whatever he asked to get the milk. She hoped his being Amish meant it wouldn't be anything illegal or immoral. She could never agree to that.

2

The minute the words left his mouth, Elam regretted them. When Katie used to visit Miriam, she'd talked nonstop, while he could barely choke out a few words. The bubbly, outgoing girl remained, although she had definitely grown up.

Elam swallowed hard and focused his gaze on the barn floor, strewn with straw. The last thing he needed or wanted was another distraction. He had enough to do just caring for the goats. But he couldn't let anyone lose their home, especially not another Amish family.

Sighing inwardly, he asked, "For soap, do I need to do all the usual testing? Separate out the sick goats?"

"We mix it with lye, so that should kill any germs. Testing's unnecessary, unless people plan to eat the soap." Katie giggled nervously.

Her bell-like laughter set off an ache deep inside. A sweet, feminine sound like that did strange things to a man suffering from loneliness. He shook off the sad memories, but nothing could erase the pain.

He had work to do and needed to get the terms set so he could return to the office. Not testing the milk would be a big time-saver. He had other conditions, though, and he had to make them clear.

"I'd like you to get your milk around back where Ray pumps the milk. If you come partway up the driveway, a smaller paved road splits off and goes behind the barn. Why don't I show you?" He motioned to the door where she'd come in.

She walked beside him, chattering the whole way.

Evidently she was as nervous as he was, but he couldn't think of anything to say. She made him as tongue-tied now as she had when they were younger. He was grateful her talkativeness made up for his silence. As they reached the small plaster shed attached to the barn, Elam interrupted her to point. "The bulk tank is in there."

He made the mistake of glancing at her. A few curly tendrils had escaped the tight rolls on the side of her head. She must have as hard a time controlling those short ends as she did controlling her tongue. He smiled at the thought.

She stopped mid-sentence and fixed him with a questioning stare. "You think that's funny?"

Oh no! What had she been talking about? He hoped it hadn't been a funeral or her family's money problems. "I, um, no, of course not."

"You weren't even listening, were you?"

The tips of Elam's ears grew hot. "I'm sorry. I was thinking about something else."

"It must have been funny. Care to share it?"

Elam shook his head. "You probably won't find it as humorous as I did."

Katie put her hands on her hips. "Try me."

"I was, uh, thinking about pulling hair back in a bob."

Katie stared at him. "I don't believe it."

"I was," he said defensively.

"What's so funny about that? And why in the world would you be thinking about it?" She looked as confused as he felt.

"I think about all kinds of things." Right now he wished he were as good with spoken words as she was. His admission made him sound foolish, and he couldn't tell her he'd been thinking about *her* hair.

Katie continued to stare him down, hands planted on her hips.

He might not be skilled at conversation, but he was good at coming up with stories. Maybe a tale from childhood would deflect her interest.

"When my older sisters were little, Mamm used to make them put their heads on the kitchen table so she could do their bobs. She twisted the hair on the sides of their heads so tightly that one of my sisters always screamed and cried the whole time. Her wails got louder after Mamm wound her hair into a bun at the back and put in the hairpins."

Her arms crossed, Katie interrupted him. "What's so funny about that? My Mamm did the same, and once in a while, she pulled hard enough to hurt."

Thinking about her hair made it hard to concentrate on his story. "I was four or five when I made the mistake of laughing at Hannah, who was three years older. After Mamm left the room, Hannah held me down and yanked my hair into rolls on the side of my head."

Katie burst out laughing. "I can just picture that. Did she give you a complete bob?"

"I didn't have enough hair for the bun part, but she tried." Oh how she had tried. His scalp still stung at the memory. "I never laughed at the girls again. Instead, I sympathized," Elam admitted a bit sheepishly.

Katie's face grew pink with mirth. "I needed a laugh so badly. Things have been so tense around the house with the bills piling up and all."

"I see." Elam still wondered at her amusement until he met her shining green eyes.

Her laughter stopped and the glow in her died, to be replaced by a bleakness that made him want to reach out to her.

Instead, Elam motioned for her to follow him. "The bulk tank's in here and so is the valve you'll hook up to." He walked up the concrete ramp and unlocked the door. "Ray insists we lock up so no one can tamper with the milk. I'll have to get you a key."

"Thank you."

He demonstrated opening the cover and unscrewing the cap. "Then you can hook the hose of your portable storage tank here."

Katie gazed at him in dismay.

"What's wrong?"

"N-nothing." She smiled, but it didn't have the brilliance of just a few moments ago.

Although speaking wasn't Elam's gift, he was good at picking up on people's feelings. Something he'd said had upset her. "You seem concerned about something. This isn't hard," he assured her.

"I'm not worried about this part. You've explained thoroughly, and there really isn't much to figure out." A small frown still creased her brow.

"Then why do you look like this?" Elam imitated her furrowed brow.

"If you must know, I have no storage tank. We have a few metal milk cans, but not nearly enough. I hadn't thought about how to transport the milk."

Elam rubbed his chin. "Before the herd got so large, we used portable tanks. I'm sure we have at least one that will fit your wagon bed. I'll check our storage sheds and pull it."

Katie nibbled on her lower lip. "How much will it cost?"

"You may borrow it for as long as you need. It's only sitting in the shed unused. So do you understand what to do?"

Katie waved a hand. "I'm sure I'll figure everything out."

"Great." Elam replaced the cap, brushed off his hands, and stood. He'd spent much of his morning milking and now showing Katie around. He had to get back to the office. He had work to do. He ushered her outside, shut and locked the door, and headed toward her buggy. "Here are my other requirements—don't disturb me when I'm in the office unless it's an emergency."

"I understand."

"I'll tell Ray about the switch when he gets the milk tomorrow morning. You can start the following day." With all the large farms

Ray collected milk from, Elam doubted he'd miss this small one. And surely Ray would understand that Elam needed to help a fellow Amish family.

"Thank you so much," Katie gushed. "I can't tell you what this means to me. And to my family."

"Glad I could help."

She headed to her wagon with that bouncy walk she'd had as a girl. He'd always been fascinated at the way she managed to put so much joy in each step. Elam shook his head. He'd better watch his own step instead of hers. If he wasn't careful, he could end up distracted. He had no time for that. Too much was at stake.

As she started off, he realized he'd forgotten to mention one other thing. "Katie," he called after her, "you can pay the same as Ray. And don't worry about paying until the end of the month."

Her jaw dropped. "For sure and for certain?" When Elam nodded, her eyes glistened with what looked suspiciously like tears. "*Danke!* What a blessing!"

Though he should have gone straight back to work, he continued to stare after her as she drove out of the driveway and down the road.

One thing he wanted more than anything was peace. Peace to concentrate on his work. If he helped Katie, his days would be anything but peaceful. He suspected from now on his life's new normal would be disruption.

Elam might not be as facile in conversation as Katie, but he liked to be precise with words. And to his mind, she spelled one huge phrase in red flashing letters like those English neon signs: *DANGER AHEAD.*

As Katie pulled away, she couldn't help glancing over her shoulder. Elam stood in the driveway, his hands on his suspenders, watching her. She hoped he hadn't seen the tears spurting in her eyes after he gave her a whole month to pay. By that time, she should have the first batch of soaps ready for sale.

She couldn't believe how kind and generous Elam had been. When he mentioned hooking up her portable storage tank, her stomach had clenched. She hadn't even thought about that. Or set aside money for it.

If she'd taken all the cash her sisters brought home yesterday and added it to the leftover money from Monique, she might have had enough for a secondhand tank, but then she couldn't pay any bills until the end of the month. Instead, she could head to the bank today and use it to pay bills. What a blessing Elam had been today! She had to find a way to thank him. And her heart overflowed with gratitude to her Heavenly Father for His care.

Dear Lord, danke for Monique's order and for Elam's kindness. I trust You will continue to provide a way to pay the rest of the bills until the soap money comes in.

Feeling lighter after casting all of her cares on God, Katie spent the rest of the ride rejoicing in the blessings she already had in her life. Doing that kept her focused on the good in her life and reminded her of many answered prayers.

When her sisters came in the door that evening, Leah quirked an eyebrow.

Katie answered her sister's silent question. "Yes, I found a supplier, but there's only one problem. I can't get the milk for two days."

"We can give up drinking ours until then. I know it's not much, but it will help, won't it?"

"Yes it will." Katie wanted to hug her sister. Leah was always ready to sacrifice for others, but Katie worried the others would disagree.

On the way to the barn to milk the goats, Lizzie was bursting with news about people she'd seen and sales she'd made, so Katie saved her news for the family dinner.

Daed peeked into the kitchen while the girls were cooking. "Leah explained about the goat milk, *Dochter*. Give us all water with our meals until you have the other milk supply."

When they came in to eat, her younger brothers started to complain about drinking water, but Daed silenced them with a stern look. He settled into his place at the head of the table while Katie sliced the meat loaf and Leah drained the potatoes. Lizzie sliced and buttered the bread.

"So who's supplying the milk?" Daed asked.

"Elam Hertzler." Katie hoped everyone would assume her cheeks had heated from cooking.

"Mose Hertzler's son?" At Katie's nod, he said, "That's pretty far to travel."

"True," Katie set the meat loaf on the table while Leah mashed the potatoes. "But he's the only one who would agree to sell me goat milk."

"I see. In that case, it was a blessing."

"It certainly was!" Katie wished she'd been a little less enthusiastic. "I mean, I'm grateful to have a supplier."

"Is he still so quiet and secretive?" Leah spooned the potatoes into a serving bowl. "He always seemed to be hiding somewhere with a book when I visited Miriam's with you."

"He was gracious when he showed me around, but I got the impression he wanted to escape back into his office." The room with the strange clicking noises. The room he'd forbidden her to enter. As soon as he'd said that, it aroused Katie's curiosity. Part of her—no, all of her—was dying to know what he did behind that closed door.

Later, as they were washing dishes, Leah sidled up next to Katie and whispered so Lizzie couldn't hear, "I didn't know the supplier was Elam. How did you feel about seeing him again?"

Katie shrugged and pretended to be paying close attention to scrubbing the meat loaf pan. She had no way to describe all the feelings roiling through her when he'd opened the office door. She thought she'd put all that behind her years ago. She was glad Elam lived in a different community. She'd managed to keep her distance when the communities got together for events like weddings and barn raisings, and as shy as Elam was, he avoided groups and conversations, so she rarely saw him. Being so close to him today, though, had opened a festering wound. Clenching her teeth as tightly as she clutched the scrub brush, Katie scoured the metal pan.

"You don't have to tell me if you don't want to," Leah said. "I just thought—"

"It's all right," Katie assured her. "I know you meant well. To tell the truth, he's changed a lot." In a good way. The cute, but stick-thin fifteen-year-old had filled out into a handsome, broad-shouldered man.

"Are you still interested in him?"

"Of course not," Katie snapped, a little too harshly. Then she softened her tone. "I promised Jonas I'd wait for him. I won't break my word."

"I know." Leah reached for the pan in Katie's hands. "I think we should rinse and dry this before you grate away all the metal."

The two of them worked in silence to finish the dishes, but as Katie wiped the counters, Leah said hesitantly, "I don't want to hurt you, but do you really think Jonas will come back?"

Katie longed to retort, *Why wouldn't he?* But her sister's question echoed the doubts that had been nagging at her since Jonas's last letter. Although Katie had been baptized, Jonas had chosen to wait. He wanted to experience the English world, and so far, after two years as a mechanic at a racetrack, he'd shown little desire to return. He loved working on and driving fast cars. His letters were filled with the thrill of screeching around the track at high speeds. Her questions as to when he planned to return remained unanswered, but Katie wanted to believe he would.

Katie finally answered. "I hope so." She tried to infuse confidence into her answer. "He's always kept his word, so I trust him to do it."

"If you say so." Leah didn't sound too sure. That was unlike her sister, who always thought the best of everyone. "Did he say when he'd be back?"

"No," Katie mumbled. The date they'd tentatively named had come and gone. "He has events lined up through the fall. Maybe he'll return during winter."

"I hope so." She gave Katie a teasing glance. "Or maybe Elam—"

"Leah!" Why had she gotten so upset with her sister, who had only been voicing some of the same thoughts Katie had been harboring?

"I'm sorry." Leah put the last dish in the cupboard. "I always thought the two of you—"

So had Katie. "I let go of that childhood dream years ago." The day Miriam had overheard Elam telling a friend he wanted to court Rosanna Stauffer.

"He's not married, is he? We would have heard."

"With no beard, he must still be single. Why? Are you interested?"

Leah busied herself wiping off the stove top and didn't answer for a while. "He's a bit old for me, and actually, I"—she ducked her head—"already have someone I'm interested in."

"Has he asked to court you?" Katie had been so caught up in her worries about bills, she'd missed this big moment in her sister's life.

"Not yet. I'm hopeful, though."

"Who is it?"

Leah bent to open the cupboard holding soapmaking supplies. "We should get started on the new bars." She pulled out a large metal mixing bowl.

Katie wasn't about to let her sister get away without answering her question. She stood, hands on hips, until the silence caused her sister to glance in her direction. "Leah?"

Her sister ducked her head. "I'd rather not say."

Katie could understand keeping hopes like that private. Her own hopes had been crushed when she'd discovered Elam intended to marry another. And she had no idea if or when Jonas would return. Finding true and lasting love seemed more a dream than a reality.

3

Elam rose before dawn so he could catch Ray Gifford while he was pumping milk. Elam was fastening his suspenders when the milk tanker rumbled into the lane. He shoved his feet into his shoes, hurried downstairs, and jammed on his straw hat. By the time he rounded the barn and entered the shed, Ray had finished measuring the milk levels and gathering the samples.

When Ray spied Elam in the doorway, surprise crossed his face. "You're out here early."

"*Jah*, I wanted to catch you before you left."

"Don't tell me you have sick goats. The company is expanding, so my employer wants all of us to find some additional sources. I'm struggling to do that, which means I need every drop of milk."

Elam hesitated. The guilt he'd been wrestling with had just increased tenfold. How could he hurt Ray to help Katie?

Ray headed out the door to get the hose from the truck, patting Elam on the shoulder as he passed. "Cat got your tongue, buddy? I didn't mean to put you on the spot. If you have a few sick goats, we can work around it."

"It's worse than that—much worse."

"That sounds ominous, but let me hook up the hose first. Then we can talk. I can't be late for my next delivery."

Elam stepped aside so Ray could exit, but stood rigid and nervous about the speech he'd rehearsed in his mind as he dressed. If he were Katie, he'd probably blurt out the facts. But he wasn't Katie, and he preferred to be prepared.

Ray followed the same procedure Elam had demonstrated for Katie yesterday to hook up the hose. Picturing Katie in Ray's place brought a mix of feelings from elation to dread.

When he straightened up, Ray met Elam's eyes. "What's up?"

His mouth dry, Elam struggled to remember the wording he'd carefully worked out, but his mind went blank.

"You had something to tell me?" Ray's tone held a note of impatience.

"I, um—that is . . ." Elam clutched his suspenders, a move he always made when nervous. Ray was watching him, and he had to spit something out. "I'm going to start selling my milk to someone else."

Ray reared back as if he'd been slapped. "Tell me you didn't say that."

"I'm sorry."

"Sorry?" Ray's voice rose in a screech. "How's *sorry* going to get me the milk I need? After I just told you how much I need milk, you go and do this to me?"

"I need to help out another Amish family."

"And cut me off just like that? After I've been coming here faithfully for more than a decade?"

"We've appreciated—"

Ray shook a fist in Elam's direction. "We have a contract. You have to honor it."

"I never sign contracts." Elam tried to stay calm as Ray's face reddened and his chest expanded with anger.

"And this is why. So you can cheat people who've been good to you."

"Actually," Elam said, remembering, "we did make a verbal agreement. A month-to-month one."

"Which you're violating," Ray pointed out.

"No, I won't go back on my word. I'll hold to the promise I made. The month ends next Wednesday. You can have the milk until then." Elam had no idea what he'd tell Katie, but surely she'd understand he needed to keep his side of a business deal. At least he hoped she would. He hadn't asked how soon she needed the milk.

"Wow, how generous. Almost a whole week to find a new supplier."

"I could help—"

"You've *helped* already. I don't need that kind of help." Ray glared at him, his face twisted with anger. "Better yet, we can hash this out in court."

"As an Amishman, I don't believe in lawsuits."

Ray's bark of derisive laughter indicated he thought Elam was lying. "You'll believe in this one when I sue you for everything you're worth."

Elam's heart went out to the man. His bluster covered his fear of losing business. Elam would have to see if any of their relatives in a nearby town could help. It would be too far for Katie to go in the buggy, but it would only be a fifteen-minute drive for Ray.

The milk tank had emptied. Turning his back on Elam, Ray unscrewed the hose, jammed the cap back on with unnecessary roughness, and slammed the outer covering. Even in his anger, he didn't forget to rinse out the tank. Then he brushed past Elam and stomped out the door.

Elam followed him out to the milk tanker. His jaw and shoulders set, Ray banged the back doors shut and marched around the truck. Elam followed him, hoping to find a way to make peace.

"I'd like to do something to make this easier for you."

As he flung himself into the cab, Ray said through gritted teeth, "The only thing you can do to make this better is to keep selling me your milk."

"I can't do that." Elam stood his ground despite Ray's fury.

"Then I'll see you in court." Ray slammed his door.

Elam stood there while Ray ground the gears and jerked to a start. Elam hadn't remembered the month-to-month contract they'd agreed on years and years ago. If only he'd thought of it when Katie was here, but being so close to her had driven all rational thought from his mind. And he'd had no idea Ray would be this upset. He hadn't meant to put Ray in a bind right when he needed new milk sources. Elam strode to the barn, his mind and heart heavy. What if he couldn't convince any relatives to work with Ray? Perhaps Elam had made a mistake agreeing to sell his milk to Katie.

After her sisters left for the market, Katie fed Daed and her brothers breakfast. Daed had found a temporary masonry job, helping a neighbor mend a stone fence, leaving Katie home with the boys. She herded them over to the kitchen counter.

"It's time to learn soapmaking. With so many orders, we'll all need to help." Although with school starting in a few weeks, she would be losing her brothers' and Lizzie's help during the day.

Aaron laughed when she handed him Leah's rubber gloves. He wiggled his hands in them to show how they flopped past the ends of his fingers. Mark slid the goggles strap over his head, but they fell down around his neck. Fortunately, they had an adjustable strap, which Katie fiddled with until the goggles stayed safely over Mark's eyes. Her sisters' safety aprons were much too large on her brothers and dragged on the floor.

Katie sighed. Buying the boys safety equipment would take more money, but she'd need their help.

"Mark, we'll need the big metal bowl and the large glass one inside it." She pointed to the cabinet that held their soapmaking supplies. "Aaron, can you get the cubes of frozen goat milk?"

While her brother headed for the propane-powered refrigerator, Katie measured out her other ingredients—coconut oil, olive oil, and tallow—and melted them together. When she set the large plastic container of lye on the counter, she warned, "This is dangerous and can burn, so you need to be very careful."

After directing Mark to fill the large metal bowl with some ice cubes, she had Aaron put the glass bowl inside. Then she poured in the goat milk ice cubes, sprinkled lye flakes over them, and stirred. Despite the goggles, her eyes teared from the sharp smell.

Mark's eyes went wide. "*Ach*, it's melting the frozen milk."

Katie nodded, "Yes, this gets very hot. That's why we put ice in the bowl underneath."

The boys watched in fascination as the lye and milk became thick and yellowish. Until now, Katie and Leah had always waited until the boys had gone to bed at night before making soap as a safety precaution. They didn't need any accidents with the boys running through the kitchen or roughhousing.

"Stay back, Aaron," Katie cautioned. "The fumes can burn your eyes."

"I have on goggles," he protested.

"They can burn your nose too. They've been bothering mine." Katie stirred the thickening liquid, searching for undissolved lye flakes.

"If this burns us, won't it burn the people who use the soap?" Mark asked.

Katie smiled at him. "After everything's combined, the lye changes. It won't harm you anymore." When she could find no traces of lye, she said, "Mark, can you pour the hot oil into a bowl?"

Aaron pushed out his lower lip and started to protest, but Katie sent him for the thermometer. "I need you to check the oil temperature for me. It needs to be exactly right or the soap will be ruined."

Once the oil was ready, Katie poured the milk solution in slowly, letting the boys take turns beating it. Then she sent Aaron for the soap molds and Mark for the dividers. They helped her pour the liquid into the molds and push down the dividers to separate the bars. After waiting a short while, they sprayed the bars with rubbing alcohol.

"How come we have to do this?" Mark asked.

Katie held out a hand to stop Aaron from over-spraying. "It prevents soda ash, which can leave a white film or even a crust on top of the soap. That doesn't look very nice."

"This is fun," Aaron said.

"I'm glad you think so." Katie smiled as she placed cardboard over the molds. "You'll be helping with lots more over the next few months."

After cleaning the kitchen, the boys picked the vegetables in the garden and painted the wooden crafts Daed had made in his spare time. Katie bustled around baking bread and pies. While the bread dough was rising and the pies were baking, she sat in a rocker in the corner of the kitchen and stitched a baby quilt for the market. As her needle flashed in and out, Katie grew teary-eyed. Would she ever have a chance to make quilts like this for her own children?

With Jonas off in the English world for so long, it seemed less and less likely. Sometimes she wondered if she'd been foolish to agree to wait for him, especially when he wasn't with the church.

Perhaps God was making her wait because she needed to be here for Daed and her siblings. Until Daed was stronger emotionally and found steady work, it was up to her to hold the family together, but she couldn't help wanting a home of her own.

Staying here by herself left her lonely much of the time. She was grateful for the work to keep herself busy. Most days she longed for someone to talk to and share with. Elam's desire for privacy made her shake her head. She suspected he'd be much happier interacting with others, so she planned to find a way to get him more engaged with people instead of hiding in that office of his, banging away.

Katie shook her head. She'd promised not to disturb him or go into the office. Even the thought of the closed door with the strange sounds emanating from it made her yearn to take a peek. Poor Elam probably would be horrified to know how much he'd piqued her curiosity. Particularly after he'd forbidden her to enter.

The apple pies finished baking, and she set them on the windowsill, punched down the bread dough, and started several batches of whoopie pies. While those were in the oven, she mixed cookie dough and set it in the refrigerator. The rest of the day, she moved from task to task, but her thoughts kept returning to Elam.

By late afternoon, she was ready to start milking the goats. Tomorrow would be a busy day. She'd be picking up the milk at Elam's. Trying to process all that milk would be a huge challenge, even with her brothers' help. They'd need close supervision for a while, which would take a lot of her time. Despite all the work, she was looking forward to tomorrow, and not just because she'd be getting a large supply of goat milk to fill her orders.

4

Thoughts of Katie and concerns about Ray kept Elam awake until late at night, and when he did finally fall asleep, he slept restlessly as dreams haunted him. Most involved Katie sneaking into the office and exposing his secret to the bishop and the church. In others, Katie trapped him into a romantic relationship. Elam couldn't decide which was the worst nightmare.

He woke later than usual, his head groggy and his eyes aching. The last thing he needed with today's deadline. Talking to Katie two days ago and Ray yesterday had taken valuable time. Time he'd needed to complete his project.

Elam dressed and hurried out to the barn. The rising sun streaked the horizon orange and pink, a sight that usually lifted his spirits, but today his thoughts were filled with worry. He was already behind on his daily chores. The goats should have been milked and fed by now. Taking care of them would keep him from working in the office. He'd be lucky to get the rest of the pages completed by midafternoon.

And if he didn't get it done on time, he might be in for another explosion this afternoon. He sighed. And he still had no idea how to settle the Katie/Ray dilemma. He'd promised milk to them both. Technically, he only had to honor his promise to Ray until the end of the month, but his conscience wouldn't allow him to drop a man who was counting on his milk supply, even if that man had threatened him with a lawsuit. He couldn't believe he'd acted so impulsively, but the tears in Katie's eyes had driven everything out of his mind and made him speak without thinking, something he never did. Elam pondered the situation while he milked the goats and cleaned up afterward, but he hadn't come to any conclusion.

He'd finished milking the goats and was heading out of the house after washing up, when a black sports car turned into the driveway. Virginia had arrived already. She'd said around three, and it wasn't even lunchtime yet.

She hurried toward him. "Darling," she said, as she wrapped him in a hug, enveloping him in a cloud of fragrance that made him choke. "It's so good to finally see you."

Elam pulled away quickly and stepped back out of arm's reach. He should have been better prepared to fend her off. "How are you, Virginia?"

"I'm sure I'll be fine once I see what you're working on."

"About that," Elam confessed, "I wasn't expecting you until later, so it's not quite ready yet."

The red lips that matched her dress and shoes pushed out in a pretty pout. "I didn't think you'd mind if I came early. We have a special invitation to one of the best parties of the season in New York tonight. I was hoping you'd come with me."

"I don't think so."

She stepped closer, and Elam instinctively shied away. "This is a big deal with lots of important contacts. You really need to be there." She reached out to take his arm.

This time he anticipated it and swept his arm toward the barn to avoid her touch. "I have goats to milk and other farm chores to do."

"You could take one night off. It'd be simple enough to catch a late train home. I'd offer to come along and drive you back here, but I'm usually tipsy after schmoozing all night."

"I don't think so. I don't have anyone to take care of the goats tonight or in the morning." He needed to steer her into the barn before his father saw him with this Englisher. "My office is right through here." He pointed to the open doorway, and she sauntered in that direction.

Before she entered, she stopped to examine the weathered paint on the brick-red barn. "How quaint." She smiled up at him. "Myra mentioned how charming your place is."

Elam wished Myra had come instead, but she was preparing to retire, so her assistant had volunteered to come in her place. He hoped he could soon send Virginia on her way.

"Goat farming sounds so romantic," Virginia gushed, although she wrinkled her nose as she entered the barn.

Inspiration struck. Elam lifted the fine-toothed rake leaning near the doorway and offered it to her. "Then I'm sure you'd enjoy mucking out the pens."

Virginia held up a hand and stepped back. "Um, no." She motioned down at her stilettos. "It'd be too difficult in these."

"You wouldn't have to worry about those getting dirty. Amish women usually go barefoot."

"Barefoot?" Her voice rose to such a shrill note that Elam winced.

"Of course. They don't want to mess up a good pair of shoes."

Virginia's sketched-on eyebrows rose almost to her spiky bangs. "But isn't there, um—you know?"

"Droppings?" Elam hid a smile. For all her liberal, big-city ways, she was acting quite prudish about simple facts of nature. "Yes, that's what you'd be cleaning out. Would you like me to demonstrate, so you can try?"

"I-I don't think so," she said faintly.

"Are you sure? Actually, it wouldn't be so bad right now. I just cleaned the pens and laid down fresh straw."

"No." Her answer came out emphatically this time.

"Shame to miss out on a chance to experience romantic country life." Elam leaned the fork back in place.

"Let's get to business." Virginia's voice sounded strained.

That was fine with Elam. "My office is over here."

"How retro," she said as he opened the door, revealing an old wooden desk and a typewriter. Before Elam could stop her, she circled the desk and reached for the stack of upside-down pages with her long, blood-red claws.

"Wait." Elam slapped his hand on the pile to hold it in place. "I'm not quite finished yet. If you'll come back around here and sit in this chair, I'll wrap it up as quickly as I can." He motioned to a straight-backed, wooden chair his grandfather had carved.

Instead of doing what he asked, Virginia backed up a few feet. "I'd enjoy seeing you at work."

Elam shook his head. He'd never be able to work with her peering over his shoulder. "I need to concentrate."

"Are you saying I'd be a distraction?" she asked with a throaty laugh.

"Yes. I work better when no one's around." Which was why he'd forbidden Katie to come in here, besides the fact that he had to protect his secret. Not to mention she did strange things to his heart.

With another exaggerated pout, Virginia rounded the desk, brushing against him as she passed, overpowering him with her cloying perfume. Some of it must have clung to his sleeve because the odor continued to sting his nostrils long after she lowered herself into the chair.

She *rutsched* with impatience as he typed. When he rolled out the final page, she breathed out a long, slow sigh. Elam suspected that, with her fast-paced life in New York, she had few opportunities to sit in silence.

Elam had no time for women who couldn't sit still without fidgeting. In fact, he had no time at all for women. Or courtship. And no one could ever change his mind about that. Not even Katie.

Now where had that thought come from?

Elam laid the paper on the stack beside the typewriter. "I'd been hoping to check over it for errors, and one of the pages needs a few corrections. Let me finish that one."

Virginia had already jumped to her feet. "Don't worry about those. That's why we have staff. I need to get the car back to the rental service and catch the train to New York." She grabbed for the stack. "I don't want to be late for tonight's event."

"I don't feel right letting a project go out of here with mistakes." For a minute, Elam thought he might have to engage in a tug-of-war with her, but she let go and sank into her seat. He slid the page he planned to correct from the stack and inserted a clean sheet of paper into the typewriter.

"Please just make the changes to that one. I promise you I'll have an expert go over the rest as soon as I get back."

He didn't answer, just concentrated on retyping everything on the page he'd laid beside the typewriter, minus the errors.

"Please," she begged as he rolled the paper from the machine, "I really do have to go." She stood and held out her hand.

Elam rifled through the pages and inserted the new sheet into its place. Then he handed her the stack.

"I can't tell you how happy I am to get this." She beamed at him, holding the pages close. "But it would save us a lot of hassle if you'd just send us your work over the Internet."

"I don't have Internet."

"We could deduct the cost from your check, and I'd be happy to pay the installation charges. I'd even buy you a computer. It'd be cheaper than these visits every three months."

"A computer would be useless. I have no electricity." He opened the office door and stepped back so she could precede him. "You don't have to come in person." He hoped that didn't sound rude. "I can always mail it."

"I didn't want to wait that long. People are clamoring for this." She patted the stack of papers. "Besides, I've been dying to meet you in person, and I'd hoped to convince you to come back with me for the party. Networking is important for your career." She shot him a hopeful glance.

Elam shook his head. Even if he didn't have goats to milk, he wasn't interested in attending a party filled with strangers. Even when he attended Amish community gatherings, he usually slipped away to read by himself. Talking to people was difficult for him, plus it was easier to avoid being reminded of what a fool he'd been over women in the past.

As they passed the goat pens, Virginia stopped short. "Don't you have milking machines for all these goats? You don't do it all by hand, do you?"

"It would be a lot to do by hand, so, *jah*, we do have equipment."

She stopped so abruptly he almost plowed into her. "Perfect. All you'd have to do is hook up the electrical lines to your office. That wouldn't be difficult."

"It might," Elam said dryly. "Our machines don't run on electricity."

"Huh? All machines use electricity."

"Our vacuum pump runs on a propane generator."

Virginia's brow furrowed. "I've never heard of anything like that before."

"Propane is how we power most of our appliances." He started walking toward her car, hoping she'd follow.

She trailed after him, her eyebrows still knotted. "But isn't that a lot of work when you could just plug things in?"

Elam shrugged. "I have no idea. I've never done it any other way."

They reached the car, and he opened the door, hoping to get her into it and out of the driveway before his Daed saw her. The only good thing was that she'd barely pulled into the driveway, so her car was out of view of the kitchen windows.

"Maybe you could come to New York for a weekend. Then you could attend a few galas. I bet you wouldn't want to go back." She placed a hand on his chest.

Elam backed up, right into the car's mirror. He was trapped, and she was swooping in for a goodbye hug. Holding up a hand to signal her to stop, he leaned back as far as he could, with the mirror digging into his lower back, to evade her.

Ignoring his motion, she moved in and hugged him.

He barely had time to register the hug or move away because a wagon rattled into the driveway. Katie. From her wide eyes, she'd seen the embrace.

Behind him, his Daed cleared his throat.

Oh no. They both had gotten the wrong impression, but he couldn't tell them who this woman was or why she was here.

Katie had hoped to get out the door sooner, but the morning was already half over by the time she helped Lizzie and Leah pack their goods in the market van, did her morning chores, and set the bread dough to rise. She debated about changing from her black work apron to the half-apron she wore when she went out, but if she'd be wrestling a milk tank onto the wagon and hauling milk, it would make more sense to have the whole front of her dress covered. Besides, she wouldn't want Elam to get the impression she was dressing up for him.

She spent some of the drive hoping not to see Elam and the rest wishing she would. Unfortunately, she'd probably need his help mounting the portable storage tank on the back of the wagon and possibly learning to use it. Yesterday, she'd enjoyed having the opportunity to stare at him while he was explaining and demonstrating. Maybe she'd have another chance today.

Her mind on that possibility, Katie turned the wagon into Elam's driveway, but stopped abruptly. A black sports car blocked her way. But that wasn't the only thing that halted her in her tracks. Elam and an English woman were locked in an embrace.

The sight made Katie sick. She'd never imagined Elam would fall for someone like that. She'd always hoped he'd fall for someone—well, like her. The childish dreams she'd harbored shriveled and sputtered out.

Katie shook herself. She'd promised Jonas. She had no business thinking about Elam this way. None at all.

She'd been so focused on her feelings, she hadn't noticed Elam motioning for her to back out of the driveway so the woman in the sports car could leave. Katie clucked to her horse and pulled on the reins a bit harder than necessary to move out of the way. She waited until the car zoomed off to drive back in.

Elam stood waiting for her. He opened his mouth to speak, but Katie didn't give him a chance.

"Who was that? Are you dating an Englisher?"

"No." Elam's short, clipped word indicated his annoyance.

But why was he annoyed? Her questions? Or being caught with an Englisher?

Elam's Daed had shuffled down the steps to stand beside Katie. "Why was that Englisher here?"

Elam ducked his head, but not before red splashed up his neck and onto his face. "She was here on business."

"What kind of business?" Katie was grateful that Mose asked the question she wanted to know.

"I can't say."

"Can't or won't?" Mose persisted.

"Both," Elam said, flustered. "There's nothing between us."

"Son, if you can look me in the eye and assure me of that, I'll trust your word."

Elam met his Daed's eyes. "I promise you, there's not."

"I believe you." A sad expression crossed Mose's face. "I wish you could trust me with the rest of the truth."

From Katie's vantage point, it sure appeared that something had happened. Would Elam lie to his Daed like that, though? Somehow, she couldn't believe he would. So what was going on? And what kind of business would he have with an Englisher—one who hugged him, no less?

"Katie?"

Elam startled her from her musing. Katie tried to pull her attention back to the goat farm, the driveway where they were standing, and her business here.

"I pulled a portable storage tank from one of the sheds," Elam said. "It's behind the barn. Why don't you check it out and see if it suits your needs?"

Was he trying to get rid of her so he could confide in his Daed? Maybe he couldn't say why the woman had come because he didn't want Katie to know. Elam was watching her, waiting for a response.

"Danke. I appreciate it." His generosity was such a blessing.

She'd only taken a few steps when heavy boots clomped behind her. Instead of talking to his Daed, Elam had accompanied her.

"You'll need my help getting it up on the wagon, if you decide on it."

"I'm sure it'll be fine. And your help would be *wunderbar*." She hoped that hadn't sounded too enthusiastic. She tried to compensate for it by saying, "I could never lift it all by myself, so I'm grateful for help." This time her words came out so stiff, they sounded like a prewritten speech. Maybe she should keep her mouth shut so she didn't keep making a fool of herself.

When they reached the tank, she exclaimed, "It's perfect!" It was roomy enough to transport large quantities of milk, but it would fit on the back of the wagon. "Danke!"

"Why don't you pull your wagon around back here, and I'll wrestle it into place. Then it'll be ready for tomorrow."

Elam's smile made Katie's heart flutter until she remembered the Englisher. Had he given her the same inviting smile? She clenched her teeth to stop her lips from curving up in response. His Daed might believe that woman was here on business, but Katie struggled to accept it.

When she turned to head toward the wagon, Elam said, "Katie, I forgot. I have some bad news for you." His words sounded ominous.

Katie stopped where she was but didn't face him. She had no idea what the news was, but she didn't want him to see her reaction.

"I, um, can't sell you the milk because—"

Katie whirled and stalked over to him until they were practically nose-to-nose. "You weren't lying, were you? You said she was here on business, and she was. You sold her my milk. I can't believe you did that." Without giving him a chance to answer—she didn't want to hear his excuses—she fled.

5

Katie barreled around the barn and ran smack into Mose. "I'm so sorry." She grasped his arms to keep him from falling. "I didn't mean to run into you."

As soon as he was steady on his feet, Mose held up one hand, while he got his breath back. When he was able to speak, he wheezed out, "I'll be fine. But what about you?"

"I-I don't know." She was still so stunned to hear that she couldn't have the milk, she hadn't processed it yet. All she knew was that her family would lose the farm. Elam had promised, but he'd broken that promise and sold the milk to someone else. She had to get out of here before the tears started. She started toward her wagon, but Mose stopped her.

"My son didn't, um, well, you know . . ." He waved a hand helplessly in the air. "Like he did with that Englisher?"

Katie stared at him blankly for a moment. He couldn't be asking if Elam had embraced her, could he? But judging from his fiery cheeks, he must be. "Ach, *neh*. It was about the milk. The milk he said he'd sell to me."

"Katie?" Elam called as he came around the building. "Please let me explain."

"There's no need." Katie hoped the coldness in her voice would freeze out any response.

"You didn't let me finish what I was saying. Ray Gifford and I are on a month-to-month contract. When I offered you the milk, I'd forgotten our agreement. I need to let him finish out the month. It'll only be until next Wednesday."

"Next Wednesday? But what will I do until then? Waiting for today was hard enough, but now I have to wait another week." Katie's eyes stung with unshed tears, and she wished she'd guarded her tongue.

"So you need goat milk now?" The kindness in Mose's tone brought a lump to Katie's throat.

She could only nod.

"They'll lose their family farm if she doesn't fulfill a large soap order," Elam explained.

Mose stroked his white beard. "How much of my son's milk did you need?"

"All of it," Katie choked out.

"I'm so sorry," Elam said. "I wish there was something I could do to make this up to you."

"There is," Mose replied. Then he turned to Katie. "I can't replace today's milk, but if you return tomorrow, I'll try to ensure that you have the amount you need."

Katie wasn't sure she'd heard him correctly. "All of it? Tomorrow?"

"I'll do my best."

"Daed, what about Ray? I can't break my promise."

"I'm aware of that, Elam. I have an idea, but right now it's lunchtime. Would you like to join us, Katie?"

"I couldn't. I have too much work to do, and I need to make lunch for my brothers."

"Tomorrow, then. You have to come anyway to pick up the milk. Why not come at lunchtime?" Mose's expression indicated he wouldn't take no for an answer.

Katie nodded her head. She'd have to prepare lunch for her brothers before she left. "All right, I'll see you then."

"Wunderbar." Mose grinned as if she'd given him a huge gift, but Elam looked sick.

As Katie walked to her wagon, their conversation drifted over to her.

"Daed, why did you tell her we'd have milk for her tomorrow? I can't cheat Ray, and there isn't enough to share."

"I'm aware of that, son. I said I have an idea, and I do."

"But we shouldn't bring her all the way out here without knowing for certain we have milk for her."

"Why don't we pray about it?"

Katie climbed onto the wagon seat, filled with uncertainty. Elam was right. She couldn't afford to take that much time out of her day. Not when she had no idea whether Mose could deliver what he promised.

But he was praying about it, and so should she. She bowed her head before she started home, begging God for a miracle.

After they finished lunch, Elam cleared the table. "So what's your plan?"

Daed explained, and Elam groaned. It meant long hours away from his office and driving all over the countryside. When he complained about the time he'd lose, his Daed pinned him with a pointed look.

Elam raised his hands, palms out. "I know, I know. It's my fault for making a promise I can't keep, so it's my duty to rectify."

That evening, he drove his Daed to visit friends and neighbors, but Elam couldn't enjoy the chats. He needed as much time as possible in the office. He was exhausted by the time they'd finished their rounds, but his Daed was glowing and excited.

"I should get out like this more often," he said. "It's helped my arthritis."

All the traveling might be good for Daed, but it wouldn't help Elam get his work done on time. If Virginia showed up in a few months and discovered he hadn't completed the next project, she'd have to return another time. That was the last thing he wanted. The less he saw of her, the better.

He wondered if English men found Virginia attractive. He couldn't help comparing all that thick makeup coating her face to Katie's clear complexion with a sprinkling of freckles across her nose. And Virginia's black hair, short and spiked around her face. Although he could only see the front of Katie's hair and a bit of her rolls on each side, he preferred hair tucked under a prayer Kapp, a sign of obedience to God.

And why would anyone wear those spiky-heeled shoes? They were impractical. How much more sensible to go barefoot and keep your feet touching the earth. He supposed some men might admire the clingy red dress, but Elam preferred modest dress on the girl he planned to marry. *Wait*. Where had that thought come from? He had no intention of marrying anyone, especially not Katie.

Yet, once again that night, thoughts of Katie filled his dreams.

That evening after dinner, Leah and Lizzie helped Katie bake more pies and breads to make up for the time she'd spent at Elam's house. Meanwhile, Daed and her brothers constructed shelving in a storage shed beside the barn where they could cure the additional soaps.

Sweat trickled down Katie's face as she bent to open the oven door. "Whew, it's hot in here."

"I'll open the windows." Leah hurried over and lifted the lower panes of the row of windows that faced the backyard.

"Danke." Katie set the bread and pies on the windowsill to cool, hoping it would reduce some of the steam in the room. She put aside a pie to take to Elam's house the next day.

"There's room on that windowsill for the pie." Lizzie pointed to an open space across the room.

Katie shook her head. "I'm keeping this separate so it doesn't get packed up tomorrow."

"You're planning to eat a whole pie while we're gone?" Lizzie teased.

"It's, um, not for me."

Lizzie pulled a batch of whoopie pies from the oven. "In that case, send it along to the market. I think we're all a bit tired of eating pie." Lizzie headed toward the counter, but slipped in some water on the floor.

As Lizzie slid, Katie used the pot holder she was holding to grab one end of the tray. When it was safely on the counter, she admitted, "I didn't plan to keep it for us. I'm giving it to someone."

Lizzie gaped at her. "You're here alone all day. Who would you give it to?"

"Our new milk supplier." Katie busied herself at the sink, washing the bowls and cooking utensils.

"But you said he isn't giving us milk until next month," Lizzie said. "Why would you give him a pie?"

"Perhaps to sweeten him up." Leah's sidelong glance at Katie spoke volumes.

"I just thought it would be a nice thing to do." Katie couldn't tell them she was eating lunch at his house tomorrow, and she hoped no one in their community would find out. They'd never believe she was going because of Mose's invitation, not to see Elam.

But aren't you?

Katie scrubbed the bread pan to erase that nagging thought. She turned her mind to Jonas. It had been more than two weeks since she'd received a letter. Long-distance courtship was difficult, especially because Jonas hadn't yet committed to the church. When he first left, he wrote almost every day, but after a year his letters dwindled to once a week. Now they came sporadically at best.

She only responded when he sent her a letter because she didn't want to pressure him. But she wrote a little most evenings, so by the time his letter came, she had a long one to put in an envelope. She had to admit she hadn't written for the past few days, not since she'd regaled him with Monique's soap order. She should write more tonight. It might take her mind off Elam. And his secretive relationship with that Englisher.

"Katie?" Lizzie said in an exasperated tone. "I've asked you twice already."

"Wha—?" Katie yanked her thoughts back to the kitchen.

Lizzie put her hands on her hips. "Did you accidentally wash the cooling racks? I need to slide the whoopie pies off the tray."

"I'm sorry." Katie hurriedly dried the cooling racks and handed them to her sister. She needed to keep her mind on her work.

Leah finished whipping the creamy filling for the whoopie pie centers. "While those cool, why don't we go out to the shed and turn out the soap molds that are ready? You'll need more molds for tomorrow." Her sister seemed to be compensating for her absentmindedness tonight.

"Good idea."

As they walked to the barn, Katie told her sisters how Mark and Aaron had helped her make soap the other day. "But we need to get smaller safety equipment for them."

"If you give me the money, I'll see if Irene could stop on the way home from market tomorrow," Leah suggested. "I'm sure the others won't mind waiting a few minutes while I run into the store."

"That would be wunderbar." Katie appreciated Leah's thoughtfulness. "We'll need everyone's help to process all the milk we'll be getting."

While Lizzie flipped the newest batches of soap from the molds to cure upside down for a few days, Katie slid later batches away from the dividers, set them on the shelves, and stuck a date marker on the shelf. Leah packed the soaps that had cured.

"I wish I could take these to market tomorrow," she said. "They sell so well."

"I know." Katie would miss the profit from the daily soap sales, but she'd need every bar to meet Monique's order.

They exited the barn, and Lizzie shouted, "Ach, Buttermilk!"

Katie raced after the goat, who'd once again managed to jump the fence. Buttermilk stood with her front feet on the kitchen windowsill, gorging on the few breads and pies left. The rest lay on the ground, trampled by her hooves. The window screens lay twisted nearby with large holes in them.

Buttermilk bleated as Katie pulled her away from the treats and into the barn. "A horse stall again for you tonight," Katie scolded. "You have to stop getting into trouble!"

By the time she returned, her sisters had assessed the damage and were looking glum.

"All the bread is eaten or crumbled," Lizzie said. "We can collect the larger pieces to feed to the chickens tomorrow."

"Most of these pies have nibbles out of them." Leah sounded close to tears as she waved her hand in the air over five pies. "I don't know if Buttermilk touched the other three, but we can't take a chance on selling them."

Katie surveyed the ground covered with splattered pies and smashed bread. "I agree." They'd had to meet rigid standards to get their kitchen inspected. If anyone got sick from eating one of their pies, they could lose their license. In fact, if an inspector knew their goat had access to the kitchen, they might lose it anyway.

Lizzie picked up the trampled pie tins. Some had dents in them. She held two out to Katie. "We'll need to replace these. They're too badly damaged. Daed might be able to tap out the indentations in the other pans."

"Put them in the sink to soak for now," Katie told her. She never went to bed without cleaning up the kitchen, but it had been a long, stressful day. "I'll do them in the morning."

"I'm sorry," Leah said. "I know you were counting on that money for bills."

Katie clamped her teeth on her lower lip, hoping her inner distress wasn't evident. She didn't want her sisters to sense the pressure she was under. "God will provide," she replied. But she had no idea how.

"At least we have the whoopie pies," Leah pointed out.

Leave it to Leah to look on the bright side. Katie was grateful for her sister's upbeat nature. "I guess we'd better package this up to sell." Katie pointed to the only pie that hadn't been touched.

"Are you sure?" Leah studied her carefully.

Katie disliked going to lunch at Elam's empty-handed, but with replacing the window screens and pie tins, they'd need all the money they could get. And almost all their income for tomorrow had been trampled into the ground outside. That along with losing Elam's milk supply for a week and the uncertainty of Mose's plans kept her worrying about making ends meet. Even more discouraging, not getting Elam's milk until next Wednesday would make her late delivering her first batch. What if Monique canceled the order?

As she fell into bed, tense and exhausted, Katie repeated her prayer from earlier in the day asking God to provide for their needs. Now all she could do was believe He'd answer.

6

A deep sense of peace washed over Katie when she woke early the next morning. She intended to leave everything in God's hands today. She was heading downstairs to help her sisters pack the van when it struck her that they had only the whoopie pies and one pie to pack. They wouldn't need her help.

Worry lines bracketed Leah's mouth and eyes as they had their morning devotions. "I fear Mary will be upset when she sees how little I'm contributing to her stand today."

"Tell her you'll bring extra tomorrow. Since I don't have to help you pack the van this morning, I can start on a few extra batches of pies and breads."

Leah nodded, but the tension lines etched into her face didn't ease. "I'll help you tonight. I know you're going to Elam's house, which will take time from your baking."

"I shouldn't be gone long." She whispered the news about the milk supply so no one but Leah could hear her. "Mose said he might have a solution, so that's the main reason I'm going for lunch today."

Leah's eyebrows rose, but she said only, "I'll be praying Mose has good news."

Katie placed a hand on her sister's arm and checked to be sure Lizzie wasn't listening. "Promise me you won't tell anyone about my lunch. You know how people talk." If word got around she was lunching with an eligible bachelor, gossip would start making the rounds, especially because she and Elam were both well past marriageable age.

Leah patted her hand. "You know I never talk about family matters. It's good Lizzie doesn't know."

"Know what?" Lizzie came up behind them, and they both jumped.

"Nothing," Katie muttered. *Nothing that concerns you, at least.* Her conscience jabbed her for the half-truth. To cover her guilt, she asked pointedly, "Are you ready to go?"

When Lizzie nodded, Katie pointed to her sweater, which was inside out. By the time Lizzie corrected it, the van had arrived. Lizzie rushed to the door to wave to the driver, Irene. Thankfully, Lizzie seemed to have forgotten the snippet of conversation she'd overheard.

Katie washed the dishes from the previous night while her sisters grabbed the containers of whoopie pies that Leah had quickly filled and wrapped that morning.

With a quick glance at Katie and one raised eyebrow, Leah indicated the pie on the counter.

"Take it," Katie said.

Are you sure? Leah mouthed, and Katie nodded.

She usually made soap in the mornings and pies in the afternoons or evenings. Today, she'd rearrange her schedule. She could still take a pie to Elam—and Mose, of course.

Unfortunately, most of the pie tins were dented. Not wanting to disturb Daed, who was adding more shelves to the storage building, Katie went to his workbench in the garage and tapped at the tins with one of his ball peen hammers until they were as even as she could get them. She hoped it wouldn't make it hard to get the pie slices out.

Once the pies were in the oven, Katie made breakfast for the rest of the family. After they ate, she completed her morning chores. Staying busy kept her mind off bills. And Elam.

Once the pies and loaves of bread were cooling, Katie changed out of her work apron. She pinned her black half-apron closed and tamed two tiny wisps of hair that somehow always managed to escape and curl on her forehead.

The mailman arrived as Katie was shaking out the dust rag. She walked to the box to gather the envelopes before Daed saw them. She'd pull out the bills and hide them in her drawer. When she removed the stack of mail and sorted through it, she separated two bills. At the very bottom of the pile, her name was scrawled across an envelope in familiar handwriting.

Katie drew in a sharp breath. Hurrying into the house, she deposited the larger pile of mail on the counter where Daed would see it when he came in for lunch. Then she raced upstairs with the other three letters. She pulled open the dresser drawer and tossed in the bills. She'd open them later. Right now, all she wanted to do was read the letter.

She settled on the edge of the bed and tore open the flap. To her disappointment, writing covered only half a page. Almost a month since his last letter, and he'd sent only two paragraphs.

Dear Katie,

I hope this finds you well. I have some exciting news! The most thrilling news in my whole life, I think. I was test-driving Brian's race car after we repaired it to be sure everything worked well. I thought I was alone on the track, so I zoomed around and tried a few fancy moves to check the steering.

When I brought the car back in, a man was waiting for me. Not just any man—a huge sponsor in the racing industry. He said he'd seen me drive before and asked me to do a few

laps while he watched. Then he offered to pay for my training.
I start racing school next week. What a dream come true!

Love,

Jonas

The letter fluttered to the floor, and Katie sat with her head in her hands. If Jonas remained a mechanic, he could come back, join the church, and still do the job he loved. But if he became a race car driver, how could he bear to give up that dream? And where did that leave her?

Jonas had been so excited, he'd only mentioned her in the greeting and first line. And he'd said nothing about their future together.

Heart aching, Katie picked up the letter, refolded it, and placed it in the dresser drawer on a different pile than the bills. She'd have to find a way to answer it, although she didn't share his excitement.

She loved him and wanted to see him happy, but it seemed his happiness depended on something that would keep him away from the church. And if it did, they could never marry. Would a day come when he was ready to give up racing and bend his knee before God?

She trudged down the stairs. What about her dreams? And the dreams they'd planned to share?

"Katie? Katie?" Aaron ran into the house, and the door slammed shut behind him.

"I'm right here," she said, entering the kitchen. "No need to shout."

He blinked. "I thought you were upstairs. Daed told me to let you know your horse threw a shoe, so you can't take the wagon."

"But I need to go somewhere."

"You'd better tell Daed before he drives off."

Katie rushed outside, with Aaron on her heels. "Daed, I'm supposed to meet Mose Hertzler about the milk supply at noon today."

"Ach, Dochter, I'm sorry."

"How will I let him know I'm not coming?"

Her Daed sighed. "You shouldn't keep him waiting. I'll rearrange my errands so I can drop you off before my appointment." The horse snorted and pulled on the reins. "He's eager to get going. Are you ready?"

Katie was glad she'd changed her apron. "I just need to get the peach pie."

Going with Daed now meant she'd arrive much earlier than noon. Maybe she could play with the goats in the barn. She had a feeling Elam wouldn't welcome her company. And with how heavy her heart was over Jonas, she'd struggle to make conversation.

She smiled at Daed when she emerged from the house carrying the pie. "Danke for taking me."

"I won't be able to pick you up until almost dinnertime, though."

Katie had no desire to be at Hertzlers that long. "Don't worry about me. I'll walk home."

"It's a long way."

"I don't mind." And walking for almost an hour was better than staying at a house where she wasn't welcome. Mose might not mind, but Elam certainly would.

On the drive, Katie tried to concentrate on the scenery and her many blessings to keep herself from dwelling on Jonas's letter and her unanswered questions. She wished she hadn't agreed to have lunch with the Hertzlers. Not only did it cut into her day when she needed to make extra baked goods, but she'd rather not see Elam so soon after her relationship with Jonas had reached a point of uncertainty.

Daed stopped the buggy briefly near the Hertzlers' house so Katie could climb out. She waited until he had pulled away before walking up the driveway.

Loud voices echoed from the Hertzlers' kitchen, along with some clanging and banging. Evidently, Elam and his father were so focused on their heated discussion, they hadn't heard her Daed's buggy.

Katie stood there, unsure whether to let them know she was here or come back closer to noon. Hesitantly, she continued up the driveway.

Mose's voice drifted out. "You need to find an Amish girl instead of an Englisher."

"I've told you several times now. I have no interest in an Englisher. Not Virginia, nor any other." His voice rose. "I'm only doing business with her."

"Monkey business?"

"Daed!" Elam said sharply. "You said you believed me."

"I do, but I worry that you're twenty-five and still not married. I had three children by your age." Mose added in a conciliatory voice, "A nice girl like Katie should be married too."

On hearing her name, Katie froze.

"Is that why you invited her for lunch?" Elam asked sarcastically.

"Would it be so bad if I did?"

"Will you please just drop the subject? And whatever you do," he added in a pleading tone, "don't play matchmaker at lunch." He sighed loudly. "Besides, Katie already has a boyfriend, so trying to pair us up is foolish."

Katie's heart twisted at his words. Yes, she'd promised Jonas, but today's letter raised concerns about whether he ever intended to return to the Amish. Even if he did, it sounded as if it wouldn't be for a long while. And Elam's tone rubbed salt into that wound.

Mose replied, "That boy is in the world and not likely to return. Besides, with him not being baptized, they should not have dated."

Guilt washed over Katie. She and Jonas had dated in secret because they'd broken the rule that couples shouldn't court until they'd both joined the church. Miriam must have told Elam about their relationship. Why would she do that? Who else had she told? But what bothered Katie even more was Mose's statement that Jonas wouldn't return. What made him so sure about that? She'd only begun worrying about it this morning.

"Jonas probably left because she talked his ear off," Elam muttered.

If he'd stabbed her with a knife, Elam couldn't have wounded her more deeply. Eyes burning with tears, Katie spun and fled down the driveway. She'd almost made it when the back door banged open.

"Katie," Mose called. "Did you just arrive? I didn't hear you pull in." A little hard of hearing, he usually talked a bit loudly, but he was practically yelling now, likely to alert Elam to her presence and put an end to their argument. His arms loaded with three disposable containers, Mose limped down the steps.

Katie, her stomach still churning, hurried toward him and offered to take the containers because he appeared shaky on the steps. He handed them over with a grateful smile and grabbed the rail to ease himself down the remaining steps.

"Elam picked up chicken barbecue at the firehouse today. I hope that's all right."

Nothing was all right at the moment. It was all Katie could do not to burst into tears. First, the disappointing news about Jonas, then overhearing Elam's true feelings about her. Both of them had dashed her hopes.

Katie followed Mose out to the picnic table in the backyard. She distributed the meals, two on one side and one on the other, figuring Mose and Elam could sit together. Before she could sit down, though, Mose sat on the side with the lone container. Katie contemplated pushing one of the other containers across the table, but Mose motioned for her to sit.

"This will balance out the table. One heavy weight on this side needs two lighter weights to keep the bench from tipping."

The last thing Katie wanted to do was sit at a table with Elam, let alone sit next to him after hearing his opinion of her, but she couldn't be impolite. The only positive thing about sitting beside him was not having to look into his eyes. Katie wasn't sure she could hide her distress if she'd had to see his face. At least she could smile at Mose, even if her heart was breaking.

Elam came out the door, carrying drinks. He shot a glare at his father when he saw the seating arrangement. Tight-lipped, he distributed the glasses and then tried to ease into his place without bumping Katie. She scooted closer to the end of the bench so their arms wouldn't accidentally brush against each other, and then bowed her head in silent prayer.

The meal was awkward, with Elam stiff and shy, and Katie struggling to keep her emotions hidden. If he thought she was too talkative, she'd keep quiet and only answer when asked a direct question. Katie felt sorry for Mose, who tried his best to keep the conversation going between two silent tablemates, so she answered whenever he directed a question her way. She was relieved when it was finally time to cut the pie.

With only a plastic knife, Katie struggled to slice and serve the pie. She could have asked for a regular knife, but Elam would have had to get up, increasing the likelihood they'd touch. Until a short while ago, she would have welcomed that. Now, she wanted to avoid it with every fiber of her being.

Mose took one bite of the ragged slice she'd dumped on his plate and closed his eyes as if he were in heaven. When he finished chewing, he smiled at Katie. "That is delicious. You're quite a talented pie baker. I expect you're equally as good at cooking meals, eh?"

His overpraising the pie made it obvious he was bringing attention to her skills as a homemaker and wife. Katie could only assume Elam was either rolling his eyes or glaring at his Daed. She longed to peek over to see, but feared Mose might interpret it as interest in his son. She kept her gaze glued to her plate and ate her slice of pie as quickly as she could. She couldn't wait for this meal to be over.

Katie finished her last bite. Despite her rush, both men had emptied their plates before she did. Grateful the ordeal was almost over, Katie set a hand on the table to keep her balance when she stood so she didn't accidentally lean too far in Elam's direction. Before she could make her move, Mose cleared his throat.

"Now that we're done with the meal, I have a surprise for you."

"For me?" Her voice squeaked. All the tension she'd been holding in had tightened her vocal chords.

Mose leaned back contentedly and clasped his hands over his full stomach. "Yes, for you. Elam has been busy all morning getting it ready."

Now Katie was totally confused. After the way he'd spoken about her, she found it hard to believe Elam had spent his time doing something for her. "Danke," she said faintly without looking at Elam.

"It was the least I could do after depriving you of milk for the next week."

Mose pushed himself to his feet. "Why don't we go behind the barn so he can show you?"

"I can't take any credit for it," Elam said gruffly. "It was all Daed's doing." He wished his father would stop trying to build him up to Katie. Daed's efforts were embarrassing and transparent. Katie had to be aware of what he was trying to do.

And his effusive praise of her pie—well, actually, what he'd said was true. It had been delicious. Elam wouldn't mind eating another piece, but he just wanted the visit to end. He'd never been this uncomfortable in his life.

Well, maybe one other time. The time he'd had to sit through Matthew Swarey's wedding to Rosanna Stauffer, feeling like a fool. Elam shook his head. He'd never make a mistake like that again. That's why being around Katie was not a wise idea.

She grasped the table edge when she stood, probably to avoid swaying in his direction. Why did that bother him? He certainly didn't want to touch her. He waited until she had risen and moved away from the table before he stood. He'd gather the trash and let Daed show Katie the surprise.

Katie must have had the same idea he did, because she reached for her container when he did, and their fingers touched. A jolt buzzed through him, shaking him to the core.

Katie yanked her hand back. Surely, she hadn't experienced the same shock he had. "I can get mine," she said, her voice shaky.

He nodded, unable to speak. So much for not touching her. When Virginia had touched him yesterday, the only feeling he'd had was nausea, and she'd been much closer to him than Katie. But it took only one touch from Katie to unnerve him.

Elam picked up the other two containers, and Katie followed him to the trash can. He lifted the lid and stayed far back as she dropped hers in, and then he deposited the others. Dusting off his hands on his pants, he motioned for her to follow his eager father, who had already begun shuffling toward the barn.

Katie walked beside his Daed and offered her arm. His Daed, who always refused help, even when his arthritis was at its worst, took it. Elam shook his head. The girl was a charmer—that much was certain.

When they reached the truck path behind the barn, Mose waved a hand at the double row of milk cans. "Elam drove all over the countryside this morning to collect them for you."

Katie stared at the ten-gallon metal cans. "Thank you," she said weakly.

His Daed's face fell. They'd both expected her to be overjoyed.

"I thought . . ." Katie gestured toward the portable milk tank he'd offered her yesterday.

It dawned on Elam that she assumed the milk cans were empty. "You do realize these cans are filled with milk, don't you?"

"What?" Her question was almost a scream. "All of them? For me?"

"Every single one."

"But, how—?"

His Daed beamed. He'd gotten the reaction he'd been expecting. "I contacted a few friends and neighbors to see if they'd each donate one can filled with milk. They were happy to help another Amish family."

"How much do I owe them?"

"Nothing. They were a gift. The milk trucks will never miss such a small amount."

Katie stood there, eyes wide, staring at the milk cans. "All of them have milk in them?" she repeated as if she couldn't believe it.

"They're full. Every one of them."

"Ach, danke! Danke, danke, danke!"

Mose held up a hand. "One danke is more than enough. We were happy to do it. Actually, if you want to thank someone, my son's the one who drove around all morning to pick them up."

Katie gazed at Elam with such gratitude he forgot how to breathe. He could get lost in those green eyes. He forced himself to look away. "It was nothing."

"You don't know what this means to me. I can't thank you enough."

"I think you already have." He wasn't sure how many she'd said, but one would have been sufficient. More than sufficient. Seeing her eyes light up when she realized the containers were filled had been the true thanks, the one he'd tuck into his memory.

All his frustrations of missing his usual two hours of office work this morning and toting the milk cans faded in the brilliance of her smile. He had to break the spell she was weaving around him. He made the mistake of glancing at her again. It was already too late for the warning flashes in his brain. Her adoring gaze sent a pang right through his heart.

7

Mose broke their eye contact by clearing his throat. "If you want to pull your wagon up here, Elam will help you load these cans."

Wagon? Ach, she had no way to get these milk containers home! "My Daed dropped me off, and I told him I'd walk home."

"Walk home? It's quite a distance by buggy and longer on foot." Mose shook his head.

Katie shrugged. "My horse needs to be shod, so I can't use the wagon. Daed had an appointment and errands to run. I suggested I could walk home. If I waited for Daed, I'd be here until dinnertime."

Mose broke into a smile. "We wouldn't mind, would we, Elam?" He glanced at his son, who remained poker-faced. From his reaction Elam didn't agree with his Daed, but Mose plowed on. "In fact, you're more than welcome to stay for dinner. You're such wonderful company—ain't so, Elam?"

If the slight tip of Elam's head was intended as a nod, he was far from enthusiastic. Katie wished Mose would stop putting his son on the spot. Couldn't he see Elam's reluctance? And hadn't he paid attention to Elam's comments in the kitchen? Katie certainly had.

Although a few minutes ago, Elam's eyes had told a different story. Or maybe she'd misread his stare. That was highly likely.

"Danke for your kind invitation, but I really need to get going. I have work to do, goats to milk, and dinner to cook."

The way Mose pinched his lips together revealed his disappointment.

"I was hoping you would stay a while. I hope you'll come again soon and visit longer next time."

"I'd like that." She enjoyed Mose's company. She might have enjoyed Elam's too, if she hadn't known how much he disliked her.

"We're not going to let you walk home. Elam wouldn't mind driving."

Elam had been gazing at the ground by his feet, but his head snapped up. He sent his Daed an irritated look.

"It's all right. I'm used to walking."

"Neh, we can't let you do that. Not when we have a wagon. Besides, you'll need to get all those milk cans home."

"Daed's right," Elam said suddenly. "I'll go hitch up the wagon." He headed to the barn.

His reaction shocked Katie. What had caused him to change his mind? Maybe he was eager to get rid of her before his Daed convinced her to stay for dinner.

Whatever the reason, she was grateful. The faster she arrived home, the more time she'd have to work. "I enjoyed the picnic. I appreciate you having me for lunch," she told Mose before trailing after Elam.

She followed Elam into the barn. "I'm sorry to keep you from your work."

He started. "M-my work?"

She gestured toward the goats and his closed office door as they passed the open barn door.

"It's all right," he said, but his eyes were wary, and he certainly seemed jumpy. What had she said to make him so nervous?

Elam's stomach had knotted when she'd mentioned his work. Had she figured out what he did? Maybe she'd guessed who Virginia was. Or had she jumped to conclusions?

He tried to relax as he pulled the wagon out of the garage, but with her so nearby, that was impossible. It did make him move one task up on his priority list. He'd planned to get a locking doorknob for the office, but hadn't had a chance to install one yet. Too many people had been distracting him from his projects lately, including Katie.

She was distracting all right, but if he were honest, he didn't mind. The mesmerizing green of her eyes, the softness of her skin when he'd brushed against it, the tingling from her touch . . . His fingers fumbled with the reins as he hitched up the horse.

Stop it, Elam!

He forced his attention to the horse and the job he should be focusing on. Elam couldn't believe his Daed had suggested he do this. Sitting beside Katie on a long ride, struggling to make conversation, would be torture.

Right now, she was silent, which was a blessing. He couldn't have answered her questions when he was struggling to do tasks he did automatically every day of his life. Despite his bumbling, he managed to get the horse hooked to the wagon. Then he drove behind the barn and backed the wagon close to the milk cans. Katie jogged over and picked up one of the cans.

"Wait, I'll get them." He hopped down from the wagon and headed toward her.

He wanted to take it from her, but her quizzical expression stopped him. She was used to handling farm work, so she'd wonder why he wanted to do it for her. As much as he disliked it, he let her wrestle the milk can onto the wagon, but he did give it an extra shove to slide it in place and was rewarded by her grateful smile.

Elam rushed to get as many cans loaded as he could, to lessen her work. After they'd packed the wagon, he climbed in and held the reins as Katie settled beside him. He registered every small move she made as she adjusted her skirt, ran a hand over the front of her hair, and checked her Kapp. He hoped he could keep his mind on the driving. One thing he knew for sure was that it would be a long ride.

"I really appreciate you doing this," Katie said.

A very long ride.

Elam nodded and flicked the reins to start the horse. He hoped Katie didn't see his Daed standing on the porch grinning, clearly elated that his matchmaking scheme had worked. Didn't he realize Katie had a boyfriend, and Elam had no interest in courting?

"Your Daed's so nice. I really enjoyed the picnic lunch. I love barbecued chicken, don't you?" Katie continued her chatter, not waiting for him to answer any of it.

Elam barely had to say a word the whole trip. He nodded or shook his head from time to time, but Katie filled what might have been an awkward silence. Instead of being bothered by it, Elam was grateful he didn't have to think of anything to say. He had enough trouble concentrating on driving with her sitting so close to him.

She had to direct him on the last few turns to her farm. Each time she pointed right, her sleeve brushed against him, sending his pulse galloping like a runaway horse.

"Where do you want me to put the milk cans?" he asked as they pulled into her driveway.

"If you can stop by the kitchen door, I'll take one inside and put the rest out here." She indicated a concrete patio by the door, flanked by a flower bed filled with pink flowers.

"Mamm had flowers like that out in our garden." He and his Daed hadn't had time to keep up with all her gardening. Seeing these made him miss Mamm's feminine touch around the house.

"I love bubblegum petunias. They're so easy to care for, and they have abundant blooms. They sell well at market too." Katie jumped down from the wagon and grabbed a milk can. "I'll take this one in."

She staggered to the door, and Elam rushed over to open it for her. The yeasty aroma of freshly baked bread wrapped him in the warmth of home and family. He missed that scent now that he and Daed bought their bread at the local farm market. Once in a while, his *Aentis* would stop by with bread.

When Katie walked through the door, Elam took a peek inside. Loaves of bread and various pies filled every counter. "Do you own a bakery?"

Katie laughed. "It looks like it, doesn't it?"

Against his better judgment, he took the can from her. "Where do you want this?"

"Right there," she said, pointing. "I could have done it."

"I'm sure you could." Elam set the can where she'd pointed and stood, breathing in the delicious fragrance perfuming the air. The barbecue dinner had filled him up, but his mouth still watered, longing for a slice of hot, fresh-from-the-oven bread dripping with melted butter. "It smells so good in here."

Katie laughed. "I'm so used to it, I hardly notice it anymore."

How could anyone not notice that heavenly aroma? Elam wished he could spend the rest of the afternoon here.

"We'd better get the rest of the cans unloaded so you can get back." Katie headed for the door.

"I'll get them." Elam hurried past her. "I'm sure you have plenty of work to do."

"I do have to package all these." Katie waved a hand toward the baked goods lining the counters. "But I'll help unload."

"You mean all this goodness isn't just for your family?" Elam teased. "I thought maybe they had big appetites."

Katie's bell-like laugh once again touched a lonely place deep inside him. He wished he could hear that beautiful sound every day.

"My sisters sell the bread and pies at the market."

"They must do a lot of baking." Elam wrapped his arms around a milk can, using his body to block Katie from reaching one.

She had to back out of his way so he could set it on the patio. "They help, but the baking's my job."

Elam backed up, again keeping Katie from grabbing a milk can. "I thought you made soap." He turned around and hefted another can.

"I do." She tried edging around him, but he slid over. "I really can help with the unloading."

"It's no problem. I'll do it." Elam set the second can next to the first.

Before he could get between Katie and the wagon, she picked up a can. "You've done so much already by gathering all this milk and driving me home. I really appreciate it. The least I can do is help unload." Huffing and puffing, she carried the can to the patio.

Elam managed to get two done by the time she set it down. He beat her to the third one. They raced for the rest, and Elam won.

"Danke," Katie said. After drawing in a deep breath, she opened the kitchen door. "Would you like to come in for a slice of pie?"

Elam had enjoyed the unloading, and he hadn't been self-conscious while they were competing for milk cans, but now he pictured sitting in the kitchen across from her, and his breath caught in his throat. He'd sit there, his mind blank, unable to carry on a conversation. Katie was still standing there, an inviting smile on her face, waiting for his answer.

"I better not." He struggled to come up with an excuse. "I need to get back to work." The disappointment on her face made him regret his answer.

"Wait just a minute," Katie said and disappeared into the house. She returned a few moments later with a loaf of homemade bread. "This is a small thank-you for all you and your Daed have done. You've both been a blessing."

"Danke," Elam managed to stutter as their hands touched. He almost added that it had been a pleasure, but he caught himself in time. He tore his gaze from her enchanting eyes and forced himself to head toward the wagon.

After he mounted, he called out to her. "I'll deliver the milk until next Wednesday. The farmers all agreed to share a can of milk until then."

"Neh, I can't let you do that."

"It'll be easier for me to swing by here after I've picked up the milk than to take it back to the farm and unload it all." Elam hoped she'd accept his excuse. It would also keep her away from the farm. That way his Daed couldn't invite her for meals, and he could keep his project secret.

"If you're sure it'll be easier for you."

Katie sounded hesitant, so he hastened to reassure her. "I'm positive."

But as he drove away, a little voice inside his head whispered that the real reason he wanted to deliver the milk was because he didn't want his Daed to see what Elam was beginning to feel. Daed's sharp eyes would detect what Elam was trying hard to fight—his attraction to Katie.

By the time her sisters returned later that evening, Katie had packaged all the breads and pie slices, frozen the goat milk, milked the goats, and baked several batches of cookies. The cookies were cooling on racks, and beef stew was bubbling on the stove.

Leah carried in stacks of molds. "These came in more quickly than Monique expected. She dropped them off this afternoon."

As usual, God's timing was perfect. Katie could only shake her head and whisper a prayer of thanks.

"That was the good news," Leah continued. An apologetic look on her face, she dumped a few coins and bills on the table. "We sold everything, but this is all that's left after Mary took her cut." Her expression brightened, though, when she saw the boxes of baked goods for the next day. "Ach, how wunderbar! I told her we'd have extra tomorrow. She'll be pleased."

"I wanted to get all the baking done before you got home, because we'll need to spend this evening making soap." Katie pointed to the milk cans outside the door. "Did you see those?"

Leah smiled. "Yes, they'll be good for picking up milk. Where did you get the cans?"

"Most of them are empty now, but they were all filled with milk."

"Filled? You got milk today? But where?"

"Mose Hertzler collected them. And—even more of a blessing—he said people donated the milk."

Leah stood with her mouth hanging open, and Lizzie, banging through the door, almost ran into her.

"Here's the bag with the aprons and things for the boys." Lizzie tossed it on the table next to the money. Then she stared at Katie. "Are you all right?"

"More than all right. Astounded. And very, very grateful to God for placing generosity in people's hearts."

Lizzie glanced from one to the other. "What's going on?"

"Are you ready to work hard tonight?" Katie asked her.

A puzzled frown on her face, Lizzie nodded. "Don't we always?"

"I mean extra hard," Katie said as she removed the boys' safety equipment from the bag. "Did you see all those cans outside? They were all filled with milk, so we have to start processing all of it tonight. Another load will arrive tomorrow."

Lizzie looked stunned for a moment, but then she jumped up and down. She grabbed Leah by the hands and swung her around, both of them squealing with joy.

Daed drove into the driveway and stopped by the door. He hopped out of the buggy and raced inside. "Is everything all right?"

Lizzie stopped her squealing, but she bubbled over with excitement. "Katie got milk today. Did you see all the cans?"

Daed smiled. "So the appointment with Mose went well, Dochter?"

"Extremely well." Katie's lips curved up at the fun she'd had with Elam as they'd unloaded the milk. It had been so much fun, she'd forgotten all about the letter from Jonas. But when Daed picked up the stack of mail and glanced through it, the shock and sadness she'd felt earlier returned.

Leah searched Katie's face. *Is something wrong?* she mouthed.

Katie spread her hands to indicate she didn't know. Leah tilted her head and frowned thoughtfully.

Daed set down the mail. "I'll put the buggy away and be right in for dinner."

Leah turned to Lizzie. "Could you set the table and slice the bread? I need to talk to Katie a minute." Then she beckoned to Katie to follow her into the living room. As soon as they were alone, Leah asked, "What's upsetting you?"

After Katie spilled out the story of her letter, Leah hugged her. "Maybe he'll realize the training isn't for him. Then he might come back sooner."

Katie hadn't thought of that. "But what if he loves it?" She'd been so focused on their relationship that morning, she hadn't thought of an even worse possibility. She sucked in a breath. "Those races are dangerous. Suppose he gets killed?"

8

Katie's fears stayed with her during dinner and put a damper on her excitement about the milk. But with everyone else so thrilled she'd found a supply, Katie concentrated on the present rather than worrying about things that hadn't happened yet. When they bowed their heads for prayer, Katie added an extra request that God would keep Jonas under His protective care and return him to the faith.

Daed startled them all with an announcement. "I was offered a permanent job today, and I'll start in two weeks."

Everyone cheered, and Katie breathed out a deep sigh. The soap money would help them get out of debt, but Daed's job would enable them to stay out.

When the conversation drifted to what Katie had done that day, she steered the conversation away from Elam and praised Mose for finding the milk.

"You know," Leah said. "If Elam hadn't let Ray take the milk, we'd never have had all this free milk. We were upset about losing this week's supply, but God worked it out for good."

"Free milk?" Daed's face darkened. "I assumed you were paying Mose."

Leah winced, and Katie rushed to explain. "I will be paying him, but Elam had already promised their milk to another company until next Wednesday. Mose said various farmers each donated one can to make up for the lost milk."

"So we've become a charity case." Daed's voice turned thick and gravelly. "You know how I feel about that."

His fierce frown froze Katie in place. She'd been so grateful to have the milk, she hadn't refused the offer. "I'm sorry, Daed."

As always, Leah played peacemaker. "The farmers actually aren't donating the milk to us. They're giving it to Mose and Elam to help them with a customer."

Daed's forehead wrinkled. "True. But we're still benefiting from the free milk."

"Why doesn't Katie just pay Mose? Then the Hertzlers are the ones accepting the charity."

"See that you do," Daed said to Katie.

Katie already knew Mose and Elam wouldn't accept any money, especially not when they'd gotten the milk for free. She couldn't argue with Daed, though.

Leah was right. What Katie had thought of as a terrible disappointment had become a blessing. Perhaps her latest fears about Jonas might end up holding a blessing. Only God knew the future.

Now that she considered it, Elam delivering the milk cans was another blessing. One she'd just realized. They might not have the money to pay the farrier for shoeing her horse for a few days. God seemed to be taking care of the little details in her life, showing her she could let go of her worries about the large problems too. Her job was to trust and be grateful for the present moment.

After dinner, Daed rose from the table and nodded toward Leah and Lizzie. "I'd like you two to wash the dishes tonight. I need to talk to Katie." He motioned for her to follow him into the living room.

At his ominous tone, Katie's stomach knotted. Was she in for a lecture for accepting charity? Or worse yet, had he heard gossip about her and Elam?

But Daed surprised her by saying, "Tonight as we discussed all the burdens you've been carrying, I realized that in addition to all your household duties, you've also been shouldering many of my responsibilities since your Mamm died." He bowed his head as his voice grew sad. "I need to take over as head of the household again."

Katie wished she could wipe the guilt and agony from his face. "Mamm's death was hard on all of us, but you suffered the most."

Daed buried his face in his hands. "There are still days when that darkness overtakes me, but I need to find a way to move through it. I've been praying God will help me face each day." Lifting his head, he met Katie's eyes. "I know you've been hiding the bills. It's time I took over the payments."

Although Daed had slowly been emerging from his depression and having a steady job again would help, Katie hesitated. Would he suffer a setback after seeing their financial situation?

"I don't think—"

"The bills, Katie." Daed's firm tone allowed no room for avoidance.

She trudged upstairs to gather the towering stack of debts. She was grateful she'd used Monique's money as well as her sisters' market pay to cover some of the expenses. Still, she worried about Daed's reaction to the foreclosure notice. She added Monique's stapled sheaf of orders to the top of the pile.

After settling into the living room chair, she handed that to Daed first. "Here's the order for the goat milk soaps, so we'll have that money coming in."

Daed studied the paper. "That's a lot of money."

Yes, it was. But it would barely cover the bills in her lap. Daed reached for the pile. His lips pinched more tightly as he opened each one. When he reached the notices of foreclosure, he groaned.

"The soap money will cover it," Katie assured him.

In a strangled voice, Daed said, "I'll talk to the bank and tax office tomorrow to see if I can work out small payments until that money comes in." Head bowed, he said in a choked voice, "I'm so sorry you had to deal with this, Dochter. I'll take care of it from now on." His eyes glinting with unshed tears, he met her gaze. "We'd have lost our home if it wasn't for you."

"God provided what we need."

"That He did. I only wish you hadn't been burdened with this. Please forgive me."

Katie's heart went out to him. "There's nothing to forgive. You were grieving." She headed out to the kitchen with a lighter spirit.

Everyone had donned their protective gear for soapmaking, so Katie hurried into hers. Normally she let the goat milk freeze overnight, but with such a huge quantity of milk, they had to do it in batches. She'd hoped that keeping the inner bowls chilled with ice would be enough to keep the temperature down. So far using slushy milk seemed to be working.

"I like doing this," Mark said as he stirred the first batch.

Katie hoped he'd still feel the same excitement by the time they got to the tenth batch. He did seem to be catching on quickly, and it would be great if he could work on his own. She cautioned Lizzie to be careful and was pleased she only needed to correct her sister a few times.

Batch after batch of soap covered the counters. If everything went this smoothly, she'd be able to fill all the orders a few weeks ahead of the November delivery.

When they finished the next-to-the-last batch, dusk had fallen and was edging toward darkness. They needed to clean up while they still had enough light to see. Katie called a halt to the work.

"I'll leave the last batch in the freezer overnight," she said. "I can finish up tomorrow morning. Let's carry these outside to the shed to cure and *redd* up the kitchen."

They each gathered armfuls of soap-filled molds and headed across the backyard. The grayness of the evening sky had deepened to almost black, making it difficult to see. Mark, as the youngest, was the most sure-footed in the darkness, so he led the way.

As they passed the goat pen, Buttermilk bleated. Then she leaped from the overhead walkway where she'd been standing. She landed in front of Mark and playfully butted him with her head. He tumbled backward, bumping into Aaron, who sidestepped to stay upright, but banged into Lizzie and they both tumbled. Soaps flew everywhere. Leah tripped, but caught her balance, and Katie skidded to a stop right behind her.

She set down her trays and dashed over to Buttermilk, who was trampling some of the soaps into the grass. Katie grabbed the goat's collar, and as she had the night before, penned her in a horse stall. If only she hadn't let Buttermilk out into the yard after milking.

At least now she discovered how the goat was escaping. They'd increased the fence height, but Buttermilk had been using the higher levels of the play yard as a jumping platform. She'd ask Daed to move the ramps to a new location tomorrow.

When she returned, Leah was near tears. "Ach, Katie, almost all of the soaps have bits of grass. Those that weren't flattened, that is."

After she and Leah stored their untouched trays in the shed, everyone gathered as much of the mashed soap and dirty bars as they could and returned to the house. Katie rolled the gaslight from the living room into the kitchen to examine the damage.

They tried to pick out the blades of grass and bits of clover, but it was impossible. Even if they could clean these soaps, remelting them would turn them brownish. Katie put her head in her hands. All that work ruined. Two days in a row, Buttermilk had destroyed their sales. As much as Katie enjoyed the lively goat, they might need to find another home for her. They couldn't afford to waste ingredients and work like this.

Katie was still mulling over the dirty, mashed soap when Elam arrived the next morning. She'd finished the last batch earlier so she'd be ready for his delivery. She hurried to the door to help him unload, but he asked her to put the empty containers in the wagon instead. As he lifted a full one out, she replaced it with an empty one. She suspected he was doing it to be kind, and the heavy milk cans did strain her back. He seemed to heft them with ease.

He caught her gawking. She looked away quickly, as if counting the milk cans left on the wagon, but her burning cheeks revealed her pretense.

She wasn't positive, but he seemed to be studying her as well, which made her so nervous she didn't lift the can high enough. It banged against the wagon, and he had to come to her rescue. As he slid a hand under the can to raise it, she inhaled the laundry-fresh scent of his shirt. That addled her even more, and she almost dropped the can.

"Don't worry. I have it." Elam eased the can from her nerveless fingers and boosted it onto the wagon. "I can get the rest." He sounded almost as breathless as she felt.

"I-I can do it." Her knees weak, Katie tried to stride toward the cans without wobbling.

"I don't mind loading and unloading. I'm sure you have plenty of work to do."

Was he trying to get rid of her? Did having her out here make him uncomfortable? She didn't want to cause him distress, but she couldn't let him do all the work alone. That wasn't the Amish way.

She'd been so busy worrying, she almost banged into him as she turned with the next can. She stepped to one side, which reminded her of last night and the soap mess still sitting in the kitchen.

"Is everything all right?" Elam stopped to study her face. "You look upset."

"Ach, it's nothing. We just had an accident last night."

"An accident? Is everyone all right?"

"Not that kind of an accident. A soap accident." She recounted last night's adventures with Buttermilk.

He set down the milk can and sat on it while she told about everyone bumping into each other. His lips quirked, but he apologized, "I'm sorry. I didn't mean to laugh at your loss, but the vision in my mind . . ."

It was rather humorous, now that Katie thought about it. Or it would be, except for the ruined soap. That sobered her. "Now I have a huge mess of soap in the kitchen I can't use. There's no way to pick all the grass out."

"That's a shame." He sat there for a moment, staring out into the distance. "Don't some soaps have bits of stuff in them? Seems to me I've seen some like that in the farm market."

Katie smiled. "Those are herbs or dried flowers, not grass."

"I see." He stood and reached for the last empty can.

"I'll get it." She grabbed for a handle at the same time he did.

He shook his head. "You don't like to let people help you, do you?"

His comment surprised her so much, she let go. He lifted the can, a look of triumph on his face. By the time he returned after stowing it, she had thought about his remark. As the oldest, she was used to taking care of everyone, figuring everything out. Yes, she let her siblings help with chores, but even there, she tried to always do the most work. And with the major things, like bills, she never shared her worries or asked for help. When Daed went through his bout of depression, she'd taken over everything, started the market business, and handled all the decisions and expenses alone.

Elam stood in front of her, shuffling his feet. "I didn't mean that as an insult."

"I know you didn't. But you were right. I have a hard time accepting help." And maybe that's why God had put her in this position—so she would learn to accept help from others. She'd needed her siblings' assistance to run the market stalls and make soap. And now she was being aided by complete strangers. That reminded her of last night's conversation.

"Daed wants me to pay for this milk." She gestured to the cans he'd unloaded.

Elam shook his head. "It's a gift. I know it's not easy for you to accept help, but we can't take money for something that costs us nothing."

"Because I have a hard time accepting help, I hope you'll let me repay you by fixing you lunch."

A strange expression crossed his face, and he started to shake his head. "I should get going. I have a lot of work to do."

Her spirits sank. They'd worked together, and he'd even talked to her a bit. Now he'd gone back to his usual tight-lipped self. He'd analyzed her, so she'd return the favor. "You have trouble talking to people, don't you?"

He stared down at the ground, but his red face showed she'd hit her mark. She hadn't meant to hurt him, and pointing out a weak spot had been a mistake.

"I do," he admitted finally. "I can never think of things to say."

"Well, if you need help with that, I have no trouble talking."

"I noticed."

She wasn't certain if he intended his words as a compliment or a criticism.

Elam didn't quite know how it happened, but a short while later, he was seated in Katie's kitchen, biting into a thick ham-and-cheese sandwich oozing with mustard and tomatoes, while getting a lesson on conversation. He sat there, staring at her as if he'd been cracked over the head with a plow shaft.

He'd never listened closely to her talking before, but he was pleasantly surprised to find when he did, she had many good insights. She didn't just talk either. She did a good job of drawing him out of his shell.

He munched on homemade pickles and chips, drank the root beer she'd brewed, and followed it with cookies still warm from the oven. Between the delicious food and the pleasure of her company, he never wanted to leave. After being in her homey kitchen with all the delicious scents, his own meals of canned soup and leftovers with Daed would seem even more lonely and tasteless.

After they'd eaten, Katie showed Elam last night's soap disaster. "I can't bring myself to throw out all these ingredients, but reheating makes soap brown."

He was pretty sure he'd seen brown soap before, but he didn't want to make a fool of himself by saying so. Then he recalled one of Katie's "talking" lessons: *Many people are afraid to say what they think because they worry about other people judging them. You can't let making a mistake stop you from saying what you're thinking.*

After wrestling with himself for a while, he blurted out, "You said not to worry about seeming foolish, so I'm going to say what I was thinking. Don't they have brown soap?"

The reaction he got was totally unexpected. She let out a shrill sound—a cross between a cheer and a yell. "Of course. Why didn't I think of that?"

He was puzzled. "Think of what? Brown soap?"

"Neh, but you're right—some soap does have a brownish color. I don't have to make all the bars scentless and yellowish. I could add colors and fragrances. Danke for the idea."

His first attempt at speaking his mind had certainly gone well, but now as he watched her glowing face, he could barely manage to say, "You're welcome." He didn't understand how he'd bantered with her earlier while they unloaded the wagon, but maybe not looking at someone made it easier.

Katie pointed to the twisted pile of soap. "I'll experiment with this batch, throw in some flower petals and fragrance, and hope Monique likes it. But if she doesn't, Leah can take it to sell at the craft stand."

She bounced on her toes like a small girl getting a surprise, reminding him of how he used to watch her skip through the meadows when he was visiting his cousin Miriam. She'd balance on logs, toss pebbles into the pond, bend down to gaze in wonder at butterflies. Every posture revealed her joy and exuberance for life.

"Elam? Elam?" The way Katie repeated his name made him wonder if she'd been trying to get his attention for a while.

Time for more truth telling. "I was reminiscing. That's one reason I'm not good at conversations. I'm often thinking about something else."

Katie blinked a few times, reminding him of Virginia's eyelashes with all the caked-on gunk. Katie's long, reddish-brown eyelashes were so much prettier. He almost said that aloud, but stopped himself in time. Sometimes speaking his mind could be dangerous.

9

On Sunday morning, Elam woke before dawn to banging in the kitchen. He rolled over and tried to go back to sleep, back to the dream of holding hands . . . with Katie? He sat up so fast his head spun. He'd spent so much time around her the past few days, and now she was invading his dreams.

At least he had no Sunday deliveries. He'd be glad when Wednesday came and he no longer had to drive to her house. He was looking forward to reclaiming all the time he'd lost. Before he knew it, Virginia would be back, and he needed to be finished with the new project.

Although he told himself he wouldn't miss going to Katie's, his heart fought with his brain and called him a liar. A long, empty day stretched in front of him, because today was an off-Sunday for their community, which meant no church service. Other than milking the goats and feeding the horse, he had no chores to keep him busy. And he couldn't work in his office either because it was still a holy day. Unless Daed wanted to visit relatives, they'd have little to do.

Reluctantly, Elam dressed and went downstairs. His Daed had fixed breakfast—watery oatmeal and runny scrambled eggs.

"You're up early," Elam said as his Daed set a plate in front of him. "Danke." Again, Elam thought it best not to follow Katie's advice to speak his mind.

"Early? Not at all. We have to hurry, or we'll be late." Daed spooned oatmeal into a bowl for himself. "I'll help you milk the goats this morning."

"No need. It's an off-Sunday." He hoped his Daed wasn't getting senile.

"Miriam is hosting church at her *Haus* for the first time since she got married." Daed set his bowl on the table and returned to the stove for the eggs. "She'd like to have some family members there, so I promised her we'd come."

Because Miriam and her husband lived in a different town, she belonged to another community, one that had services today. "It would have been nice to know ahead of time rather than on Sunday morning."

Daed rubbed his forehead. "I told you twice this week, but you were off in dreamland every time I tried to speak to you." With a sly smile, he added, "I think it has some connection with those milk deliveries of yours."

"It has nothing to do with that." Elam spoke more harshly than he'd intended. "I'm sorry, Daed. I didn't mean to snap at you, but you're jumping to conclusions."

"I'm not so sure about that." His egg plate joined the oatmeal bowl, the twinkle in his eyes undiminished.

"I am." Elam emphasized the words.

Daed dropped into his chair at the head of the table and closed his eyes. Elam did the same. When he lifted his head, he hoped for a change of topic. He tried to remember Katie's suggestions for starting conversations, but nothing came to mind.

His Daed picked up a forkful of eggs, which slithered through the tines. "I guess we need a spoon for these."

Elam seized on that. "A spoon's a good idea." If he were Katie, he'd probably find a way to talk about silverware or eggs.

"I've noticed your delivery times took longer the past few days."

"Umm." Elam hoped a noncommittal reply would stop the inquisition. He shoved a spoonful of oatmeal into his mouth as double protection.

"So how are things going between you and Katie?"

Elam choked on the mouthful. "Me and Katie?" He set down his spoon and met his Daed's eyes. "There is no 'me and Katie,' and there never will be. Can we please drop this topic?" This time he'd spoken his mind, but his heart begged to differ.

Daed waggled his bushy eyebrows as if he didn't find the denial convincing. All he said was, "Hmmm."

After shoveling in his food as quickly as he could, Elam pushed back his chair. "I'll start the milking. We'll need to leave before seven thirty if we want to make it on time."

"I'll clean up the dishes and be right out to help."

"Danke." Elam hurried to the barn, hoping to finish as much of the work as possible before Daed joined him. Milking was difficult for him with his arthritis, so Elam wanted to spare him. And perhaps spare himself from another inquisition.

Being in the barn reminded him of Katie. If he were honest, almost everything reminded him of Katie these days. He needed to get her off his mind. He fed the goats, but as he milked, his mind wandered back to their lunchtime conversations. He enjoyed their talks. He wished he hadn't been so enamored with her when he was younger that he'd been too shy to speak to her. He'd used his books as an excuse to avoid approaching her.

Elam shot to his feet. *Katie and Miriam.* They'd been best friends, and they were still in the same church district. His fists knotted. That explained why Daed had talked about her at breakfast. Of all the scheming, conniving . . .

Daed's matchmaking had gone far enough. Elam had made it clear he wasn't interested in Katie, yet Daed kept finding ways to throw them together.

His Daed shuffled into the barn, more bent over than usual, and all the fight leaked out of Elam. How could he be angry with the man who loved and cared for him? Yes, Daed was mistaken about Katie, but he was doing it out of love.

"I'll take care of the goats, Daed. You go back in the house and put your feet up for a while." Sitting on those backless benches for hours during the sermons would be hard on him. In their church, they usually seated him in the front row in a cushioned folding chair, but the members of this church district would be using those designated chairs.

"Thanks, son. I'm feeling a bit stiff this morning, but we'll need to hurry."

"I will. One question before you leave, though." Elam turned to face his Daed to see his reaction. "When did Miriam invite us?"

"Three days ago."

"I see. And did you happen to know Katie's part of that church district?"

His Daed tried to feign surprise, but he couldn't quite pull it off. He stared down at the floor. "Yes," he said after a few seconds. "I hoped . . . well, a father wants to see his son married."

"You don't trust me to pick someone?"

"I was worried about that Englisher, and I mentioned it to my sister. She agreed Katie would be a better choice. Miriam invited us the next day."

"Everyone seems to be forgetting Katie has a boyfriend."

Daed shook his head. "She can't marry someone who's not with the church."

Elam moved down the row. "I'm sure he's planning to be baptized, or she wouldn't be waiting for him."

Daed limped toward the barn door. "Sometimes love can be blind."

Elam wasn't sure if that parting shot had been directed at him or Katie.

Katie dragged herself downstairs in her church clothes. Leah had talked to Monique yesterday at the market, and the spa owner had agreed to assorted batches, some with herbs and scents, so Katie had stayed up after everyone had gone to bed and reprocessed all the batches Buttermilk had trampled.

Mark and Aaron thundered down the stairs. Katie caught Mark by the suspenders as he raced past.

"Hold on a minute." She straightened his wrinkled collar and smoothed it flat. "Daed's pulling the buggy around, so go get your hats on."

Lizzie raced down the stairs, followed by Leah, who descended demurely. Katie had promised Miriam to come a little early. Her friend needed extra help. Katie supposed the first time you held church in your house, it would be especially nerve-racking. It would be even if it wasn't her first time. Katie was always edgy when they hosted. She wanted everything to be clean and ready. Luckily, their turn occurred only about once a year.

As they packed into the buggy, Katie passed the empty milk cans. She wouldn't see Elam until tomorrow. She'd gotten used to their lunchtime visits. The one on Friday had stretched into midafternoon. And Elam had said he'd like to see the soapmaking process on Monday. Perhaps he'd spend most of the afternoon.

She hadn't convinced him to speak freely, but he was improving. He still lost track of conversations when he drifted off into thought, but she was getting used to that. Sometime she hoped he'd be comfortable enough to share those thoughts with her.

By the time they arrived and all the women in Miriam's kitchen had greeted Katie, the two of them had no time alone. But Miriam whispered in passing, "I hope you like today's surprise."

Katie had no idea what Miriam meant, but the service was starting, so she hurried in to sit on the women's benches with her sisters. She smiled at Daed and her brothers, who were seated across the room from them. Her tired eyes scanned the row beside them, and Katie jolted upright. What were Mose and Elam doing here?

Family members often visited each other's churches, but she'd never seen them here before. Was this the surprise Miriam had mentioned? If so, Katie would classify it more as a shock than a surprise.

Elam didn't look in her direction, but Mose's smile reminded her of Aaron's when she caught him sneaking cookies—a little charm overlaying plenty of guilt. She'd rather not encourage him in his matchmaking, so she tempered her smile with a rebuke in her eyes.

Katie had trouble keeping her mind on the singing and sermons. But Elam's presence kept her from dozing off. Whenever she glanced at him, which was more often than she should, he never met her eyes. Yet several times she'd peeked at him from the corner of her eye to see his gaze fixed on her. The second he noticed her gaze, he glanced away quickly without acknowledging her.

After the service was over, Katie hurried to the kitchen to help carry out the food, while the men converted the benches into tables. Miriam cornered her in the kitchen.

With her back to everyone, Miriam whispered, "So?" Her broad grin and raised eyebrows made it obvious she was dying to hear some news.

Katie didn't want to give her a mistaken impression. She must think something was going on between her and Elam. "It was nice to see your *Onkel* and cousin here today." Katie kept her voice neutral. "I can't wait to hear. What's the surprise?"

From Miriam's crestfallen expression, she'd been expecting a different reaction. "I need to get the food on the table. Could you take the church spread? Mamm and some other ladies are taking care of the lunch meats." Miriam picked up two full pitchers and motioned with her chin to the door.

Many of the men sat at the tables already. The women would eat next. Katie's eyes automatically sought out Elam, but she averted her gaze before Miriam or anyone else noticed.

Several young married men seated beside him were laughing. One slapped Elam on the back and said loudly enough for her to hear, "Congratulations on finally dating. Your Daed said you've been courting Katie Kurtz."

Elam's words cracked through the air like a whip. "Daed's mistaken. I'm not courting Katie. And if I ever do choose a girl to marry, Katie Kurtz would be at the bottom of the list."

"Ach," one of them said. "There's Katie."

Although Elam had just sliced her heart to shreds, she swished past their table, keeping her chin up and a smile pasted on her face. She'd never expected Elam to court her, but she'd thought they were at least friends. Maybe teaching him to speak his mind hadn't been such a good idea if his thoughts were so cruel.

She blinked and swallowed hard to hold back the tears threatening to spill from her eyes. With shaking hands, she set the peanut butter spread on the table and clenched her fists in the folds of her apron to maintain control before she turned toward Elam's table again.

Then she did one of the hardest things she'd ever done—looked straight at Elam and the others at the table. Elam had his head down, his hand across his forehead, shielding his eyes as if he were ashamed. The young men surrounding him blushed or avoided her gaze. Katie tried to keep her face neutral and expressionless, hoping her eyes didn't betray the depth of her pain.

When they returned to the kitchen, Miriam pulled her aside and hugged her. "I'm so sorry. I'm sure my cousin didn't mean what he said. He was only trying to stop the teasing."

He could have ended it by saying he had no interest in her. That would have stung, but to say she was at the bottom of the list!

If she let the tears come, they might not stop. Keeping her back to the room, she closed her eyes and pressed two fingers to the bridge of her nose.

"Do you want to go upstairs to my bedroom?" Miriam asked.

Katie shook her head. She wouldn't run away, but coming so soon after Jonas's recent letter, Elam's rejection had been doubly painful and made her wonder if anyone would ever want to marry her.

Miriam led her to the farthest corner of the kitchen and opened the pie safe. "Why don't you stay here in the kitchen and cut the pies?"

Katie squeezed Miriam's hand and managed a hoarse, "Danke." She pulled pie after pie from the narrow wooden shelves, slid the knife through crust and filling, and then handed it off to one of the women to carry out to the table. Each cut she made in the pie reminded her of Elam's cutting rejection.

She turned to hand off the next pie and met the gentle gaze of Miriam's mother, who put a hand on her arm. "Mose tells me you and Elam are courting. I'm so happy for both of you. You make a lovely couple."

Nearby, Anna stopped slicing bread. "Ah, so that explains why Elam's wagon has been parked in your driveway for hours. Bertha mentioned she saw it twice last week."

Katie hoped her eyes didn't show the way she felt—like a startled deer, frozen in place. *Say something, Katie. Explain. Defend yourself.* But for the first time in her life, she was at a loss for words.

Elam excused himself from the table and walked outside, feeling sicker than he ever had in his life. He had to find Katie to explain and apologize, if she'd ever speak to him again. But he couldn't do it here at the church meal because the women ate separately from the men.

He'd spent his life trying never to injure anyone in word or deed, but what he'd said about her was unforgiveable. Even worse, it was a lie. He needed to confess that to the men at the table, but he owed Katie the first apology. Perhaps he could wait by her carriage and catch her before she got in.

A hand descended on his shoulder. "I believe we need to have a talk, young man."

Elam faced the man, and his heart sank. Katie's father. Judging from his expression, what he had to say wasn't good. Had he heard the insult to Katie? If so, Elam deserved whatever tongue-lashing he had coming.

"It has come to my attention that you've been calling on my Dochter when no one else was at home."

What could he say in his defense when that was true? He hadn't thought about it that way. In fact, he hadn't been thinking at all.

"Katie says you were delivering milk—something for which we were all grateful, especially since her horse threw a shoe," David Kurtz went on.

"Jah, I was." And that's all it had been. That and some friendly conversation.

"How long would you say it takes you to load and unload a wagon?"

Elam answered honestly. "Fifteen or twenty minutes."

"That's what I'd estimate too." David frowned. "So why was your wagon parked in the driveway for hours?"

"We were talking."

"I haven't spoken to Katie yet, but I know my Dochter well enough to know she wouldn't do anything wrong. I am, however, concerned about her reputation."

"I'm sorry. I didn't think about that." It had never occurred to him that people were monitoring how long he parked in a driveway. Perhaps if he'd been doing something wrong, he would have considered the consequences.

"Jah, well, the Bible warns to stay away from all appearances of evil. So I hope you'll think next time." Katie's Daed exhaled a long breath. "To help with that, I've talked to your Daed. Katie's wagon will be fixed by Monday. She'll come to your house, where Mose has promised to be present for the loading."

"I understand. In the future, I'll try not to do anything that might harm your daughter's reputation." Although he just had this afternoon. He hoped Katie's Daed didn't hear about that. He'd already done enough damage to Katie and her reputation.

10

Elam had no chance to apologize to Katie after church. Her father hustled her out to their carriage, and Katie seemed relieved to go, which was all Elam's fault.

He did apologize to everyone at the table who'd heard his remarks. He also admitted he'd lied about Katie being last on his list. He explained the two of them were friends, but not courting.

On the way home, his Daed gazed at him with sad eyes but didn't say a word. If Daed knew, then everyone else had probably heard. Not that his opinion would have any effect on people's views of Katie, but it still never should have been said. And it had hurt her feelings.

The rest of the evening, his comments haunted him. Katie's advice about saying the first thing that popped into one's head might work for her, but it had backfired on him. Maybe God had created him tongue-tied for a purpose, so he'd have to think long and hard before he made any statements.

Too upset to eat, he fixed soup for Daed and went to milk the goats. Then he went up to bed early, only to toss and turn all night. When he rose in the morning, he did his chores silently and headed off to collect the milk.

The empty cans rattling in the back of the wagon brought memories of Katie. The fun they'd had talking—well, mainly her talking and him listening. The laughs they'd enjoyed. His carelessness had crushed all hopes of a future together.

He shook his head. All along he'd been adamant about not being interested in Katie. About not wanting to get married. So why was he lamenting the lack of a future?

Somehow, despite all his protests, she'd gotten through his defenses. That realization stunned him. He also had to face the fact that, if he were honest, Katie wasn't at the end of his list—she was at the very top. Number one.

Driving back home after he'd collected the milk, his stomach roiled. A knot of dread closed off his throat. What could he say to her to make things right between them? He rehearsed several speeches, but they all sounded like excuses instead of apologies. A simple, "I'm sorry. Please forgive me," wouldn't erase the words from her mind. He had to let her know he lied without giving away her true status in his heart.

He went into his office, but he couldn't concentrate. He rolled a fresh sheet of paper into the typewriter, but no words came. The only words forming in his mind came together as an apology for Katie.

Katie dreaded pulling into the Hertzlers' driveway. Her stomach ached, and her eyes stung with unshed tears. She wished Daed hadn't insisted on Mose keeping an eye on her. She wasn't sure how she'd react to seeing Elam.

Neither Mose nor Elam were outside when she drove up the back driveway. The milk cans were in the same location as before. Maybe she could load them without either of them seeing her. That would be a blessing.

She wrapped her arms around the first can. It was much heavier than she remembered. Perhaps because Elam had handled the full ones, while she did the empty ones. They'd joked and laughed together too, which made the burdens lighter. Her eyes blurred with tears. She'd thought they were friends. They couldn't be anything more, not while she was promised to Jonas, but Katie's attraction to Elam had been growing.

She shook her head. No, she'd always been attracted to him, even when they were young. She'd look for opportunities to talk to him, even if it meant interrupting his reading. But that childhood crush had matured, and the more time she spent around Elam, the more he edged Jonas from her mind.

She groaned as she hefted the milk can onto the wagon. She missed Elam's help.

But as much as it hurt, she wouldn't have that ever again. His words had destroyed her. If any good came from them, though, they made her realize how wrong their—no, her—growing attachment was. She hadn't realized the relationship between them had been so one-sided. But his cruelty had reminded her she had a promise to keep to Jonas.

As Katie bent over to pick up the next milk can, Elam's voice startled her. "Let me get those."

"I don't need any help." Her tone was clipped and cutting. She kept her back to him so he couldn't see her teary eyes.

"Katie, I'm so sorry. I'd like to explain—"

"There's no need to explain. Just go away and leave me alone."

"But I didn't mean—"

She held up a hand to stop him. She didn't want to hear what he did mean. What she'd heard had been enough. And if he planned to deny what he said because he felt guilty that she'd heard it, she didn't want to hear any lies.

"Please, Katie. Won't you—"

"No, I won't do anything. Not listen to you. Not accept your help. Not—" She stopped just before she said *love you*. Not only because she couldn't admit that to him or herself, but because it was true.

Despite all her denials, despite all her promises to Jonas, she'd fallen in love with Elam.

"Katie, I'm sorry. Please let me apologize. Explain." Elam came up beside her and lifted a milk can. "You know I'm not good with words."

His pleading tone touched her, but she hardened her heart. In the most savage tone she could imagine, she spat out, "All I want from you, Elam Hertzler, is for you to leave me alone. Stay away from me. When I come for the milk, I don't want to see or talk to you."

"I understand," he said, his voice quiet. "I'll just help you load these, and then I won't bother you again." The can in his arms clanked onto the wagon.

She had to keep her back to him, or she'd crumble. "No, you don't understand. I can handle the milk cans alone. The best apology you could give me is to go back into your office and not come out while I'm here."

He ignored her and picked up another can.

"I mean it." She struggled to keep her voice firm. "I don't want your help. I don't want to see you or be near you again."

"I see." He put the milk can on the wagon. "I won't bother you again." He turned and headed into the barn.

Katie wanted to cry out for him to stay, but she clamped her lips together and blinked away the moisture in her eyes. She waited until he was inside the barn to pick up the next can. This one seemed even heavier than the first one. Perhaps because sending Elam away had sapped all her energy.

She was wrestling the can onto the wagon when Mose called out, "Katie, I didn't hear you drive in." He limped down the steps. "Let me help you with those."

"I can do it." Katie tried to infuse a note of certainty into her voice. On an ordinary day, maybe she could, but after yesterday, she could barely force one foot in front of the other.

Mose slid a hand under the can she was holding and helped her slide it onto the wagon bed. Then, grunting and groaning, he tried to pick up another can. He panted as he walked the few feet to the wagon.

"Please, I can do it myself." She didn't want to insult him by telling him he shouldn't be lifting heavy objects, but she feared for his health.

He grimaced and held his back. "Where's Elam? He should be out here helping."

"No, please—"

But Mose yelled, "Elam, we need your help out here!" Then he bent to lift another milk can.

Elam rushed out of the barn so fast, he must have been standing by the door. "Daed," he said sharply. "You shouldn't be carrying those cans. I'll get it." He hurried over and took the can.

"I can help," Mose insisted, though his face was red and his forehead was covered in sweat.

"Think about your heart," Elam reminded him. "Why don't you stand over there and supervise?"

Mose took Elam's advice and moved under the shade of an old oak, watching them. Once again, she and Elam were locked in a competition to see who could load the most milk cans. Only this time, it wasn't a friendly race. They both wanted to do it as quickly as possible so they could get away from each other.

When the last can went into the wagon, she thanked them without looking at Elam, waved goodbye to Mose, and hurried into her wagon. She couldn't get out of there quickly enough.

Elam stood, staring after the wagon, wishing he could call Katie back and explain. But what could he say to erase the damage he'd inflicted? He couldn't tell her the truth.

"Don't you have work to do?" Daed's knowing grin only added to his sorrow.

A short while later, Elam inserted a sheet of paper into the typewriter. He tried several times to work on his project. When he first met Katie, he wanted her to leave him alone. All he wanted was peace to concentrate on his work and to think and create away from her. Away from the memories of his childhood crush and youthful failures. Away from her bubbly chatter. Now all he wanted was to hear her voice, see her smile, and spend time with her.

He'd predicted she'd disrupt his life, and she had. But not in the way he'd expected. He never thought he'd prefer being with her to working on his dream projects. But he had only one problem. He'd destroyed their budding relationship out of embarrassment and self-defense.

She had said his fear of talking was a form of self-defense. He didn't want people to know about him because he was afraid of being judged, mocked, or rejected. She was right about that. As a private person, he hated having his deepest feelings exposed. When his cousins and their friends teased him, they'd hit on a deeply hidden secret, one he hadn't even wanted to admit to himself, let alone a whole tableful of people. He'd thrown out the most far-fetched excuse he could think of to conceal the truth. He'd only wanted to stop the teasing. The last thing in the world he ever wanted to do was hurt Katie. If only he'd found a different way of guarding his secret.

He had to find a way to explain that he hadn't meant what he said, and apologize. But how could he do that when she wanted nothing to do with him? She'd ordered him to leave her alone. He didn't blame her. He wouldn't want to be around someone who'd said something that cruel.

He wanted to see her, but he also wanted to respect her feelings. It was the least he could do after humiliating her so publicly. When she'd told him to go, he felt like his heart was being ripped from his body. Walking into the barn had taken all his willpower. Maybe if he gave her some time to get over it, she'd be willing to hear his apology.

Shaking off his thoughts about Katie, he forced himself to start his project. He'd only managed to type a few words before thoughts of her intruded. He couldn't get her off his mind.

He unrolled the paper in the typewriter and ripped it out. Then he put in a clean sheet and began typing. He typed all afternoon, but hours later, he'd accomplished nothing on his project. The trash can beside his desk overflowed with crumpled papers.

Every single one of them an attempt at an apology.

But how could he apologize for something so awful? If he tried to explain in person, it would come out awkwardly. Usually he was fluent on paper, but today no words flowed from his fingers.

When he spoke, the words and sentiment came from his mind. When he wrote, they came from his heart. But he'd been trying to write an apology without exposing his heart.

After another sleepless night, Elam collected the milk cans for Katie and drove home. Then he taped a simple apology—one with no explanations or excuses—on one of the metal cans and retreated to his office. He longed to see her face when she read it, but she'd asked him to leave her alone, so he'd respect her wishes.

Once again, nobody was around when Katie drove in to pick up the milk the next day. Seeing Elam would be much too painful, so she hoped he'd take yesterday's ultimatum and not show up. She was grateful Mose was hard of hearing and hoped he wouldn't glance out the window. He'd be sure to call Elam again.

As she hopped out of the wagon, the wind blew a small piece of paper in her direction. She disliked littering, so she trapped it under her shoe, crumpled it without looking at it, and discarded it in Mose's outdoor trash bin. Then she returned to the row of milk cans and began transferring them to her wagon.

Red-faced and groaning, she hoisted each can, alternating between dreaming Elam was working beside her and praying he wouldn't come out. As she set the final can in place, she heaved a huge sigh. She'd done it. She hurried to her wagon and clucked to her horse, who trotted down the driveway. After they turned onto the road, she held in the cheer trying to escape from her mouth. She didn't want to alert Mose or Elam to her presence.

After picking up the milk cans at Elam's the next day, Katie baked up a storm and threw herself into the soapmaking frenzy, leaving herself little time to think about him. Her sisters were thrilled with all the extra baked goods, but Leah studied her with concern.

"Are you all right?" Leah asked as they packed another box for market.

"Not really," Katie confessed, but when Leah questioned her, Katie was reluctant to reveal her heartbreak. She'd told no one of her feelings for Elam. Leah and Miriam knew of her childhood crush, but she'd been careful not to share her hopes that the friendship she and Elam shared—*used to share*, she corrected herself—could blossom into more.

"Is the letter from Jonas still worrying you?"

"A little." Now that Leah had reminded her of it. But the past few days, Katie had forgotten all about Jonas and the letter. She had no right to pine for Elam when she was promised to Jonas.

"Take it to the Lord in prayer," Leah advised.

"Thanks for reminding me, Leah." That's exactly what she needed to do. Although she'd prayed about Jonas, guilt had kept her from unburdening her heart over Elam. "Can you finish the packing? I'd like to go upstairs for a while."

Leah reached out and patted her arm. "Of course. You'll feel much better once you do."

Katie went to their bedroom and shut the door. Then she knelt beside the bed and poured her heart out to God. When she rose from her knees, she felt lighter. Her heart was still fragile, but her focus needed to be on doing God's will, even if that meant living a single life. She resigned herself to that possibility.

11

Elam had hated staying in his office when Katie was outside struggling to lift the heavy milk cans the past two days, but he'd gripped the chair arms and remained in his seat. She'd never responded to his note, so she must still be upset, and understandably so. He almost went out to ask if she wanted help loading the portable milk tank on her wagon. She'd need it tomorrow for pumping the milk. But he decided to wait until the morning.

Then late the previous evening, she and her Daed had returned the empty cans, and her Daed had loaded the portable milk tank onto her wagon. Elam's Daed had already gone to bed, and Elam was still trying to make a start on the project for Virginia. Enough moonlight filtered through the small window that he could type, but he couldn't read the words on the paper. That might be for the best. Last night, he'd had a feeling when he saw this page in the morning light, it would be filled with gibberish, or worse yet, his unrequited feelings for Katie. And it was.

When she and her Daed arrived, he'd abandoned his typing altogether to watch her. If she wondered why he had so much trouble talking, she only had to remember the terrible things that occurred when he did speak. Telling Matthew he was interested in Rosanna had ended with his best friend marrying the girl he'd intended to court. Trying to defend himself from teasing at the church meal had cost him Katie's friendship—a much deeper and more painful loss. From now on, he vowed to keep his mouth shut.

Never again would he try for romance. Losing out again had taught him a heartbreaking lesson. Love and marriage were not for him. He'd decided that after Rosanna, and he regretted allowing Katie's charm to change his mind. He had his work, and he'd pour all his passion into his projects. That, at least, was safe. As long as nobody discovered what he was doing.

For the first morning in a week, he could head straight into his office after milking the goats. No traveling all over the countryside picking up milk cans. No smiling face to greet him when he delivered them. No working side by side to load and unload the wagon. No more—

Elam hunched over the keyboard and forced himself to concentrate. Katie wouldn't need help today. She'd pump the milk into the portable milk tank, and he could stay in here at his desk to avoid her.

For the first time since she had entered his life again, he forced himself to concentrate, and before he knew it, he was completely consumed by the new project. Creative thoughts spilled from his brain so quickly his fingers could barely keep up. He was thrilled about the direction the work was going and worried his ideas would trickle to a stop after the first gush, but they continued to flow.

When her wagon rattled past the tiny window, the sound barely registered. He was fully submerged in the work. Work was a good antidote to pain, and Virginia's three-month deadline kept him focused. He refused to let outside noises or messy emotions distract him from completing this project.

Katie hadn't explained to Daed why she needed him to load the portable pump, but he asked no questions when she suggested going after dark. This morning, before he left for work, Daed had checked the pump and assured her it was in good working order.

After she hooked up the wagon, she ran her hand over the big white metal tank, grateful for Elam's generosity. She tore her thoughts away from him. She refused to dwell on the dreams she'd harbored.

She had work to do, and she needed to get started. She assured herself the fluttering in her stomach was nervousness about starting a new venture and using equipment she'd never tried before. But the closer she came to the Hertzlers' farm, the worse the fluttering grew. Now a whole flock of birds flapped their wings inside of her, and her throat closed off.

All right, so maybe it wasn't only pumping milk for the first time that had her in a panic. Her jumpiness eased a little when she reached the back of the barn without seeing Elam or Mose. Going through the steps Elam had taught her would be painful, but she'd rehearsed them in her mind so many times last night, she was positive they'd go smoothly.

She parked the wagon at the best angle to access the storage shed. Then she leaped down, eager to begin and to get out of there as quickly as she could. But the shed door was locked. Elam had promised to give her the key, but they'd both forgotten about that. Now she'd have to see him.

The butterflies flapping around in her stomach changed into giant birds of prey, beating their wings and pecking at her insides. *Lord, please give me the courage to face him.*

The Bible directed them to forgive those who hurt them, and after wrestling with her pain last night, she'd forgiven him. But she'd always feel uncomfortable around him, knowing his true feelings. The exasperated looks he'd given her all those years ago whenever she interrupted his reading should have given her a clue. Evidently, his feelings hadn't changed, but as an adult, he'd learned to hide them behind a mask.

Today, on her first day pumping milk, she already had to break one of his rules. He'd asked her never to disturb him when he was working in his office. If she didn't, though, she couldn't get the milk. Doing her best to ignore her nerves, she entered the barn.

Rapid clicking issued from within the office. She stood for a few moments, taking deep breaths, before tapping timidly. Then she waited, but received no answer. The furious clacks continued unabated. Maybe he hadn't heard her. Gathering her courage, she knocked a little harder. Again, no answer—only that odd noise. Maybe he was ignoring her, the way she'd told him to. All she wanted to do was flee, but she needed the milk. Pinching her lips together, she banged on the door.

"Who's there?" The exasperation he'd exhibited as a child was clear in his voice.

"It's Katie," she said hesitantly. "The door to the milk room is locked."

"Are you sure? I told Ray to leave it unlocked." Impatience seeped into his words. "Maybe he just closed the hasp without locking the padlock."

Was it her imagination, or was he treating her like an idiot? "It's definitely locked."

A loud sigh escaped through the walls. "Just a minute." A few more clicking sounds, and then a chair scraped across the floor. He opened the door only wide enough to slip through. Curiosity kept Katie from glancing at him. What was he doing in there to make that strange sound?

His body blocked her view of the room, and he slammed the door shut before she could get even a glimpse. A bit disappointed not to see inside, she glanced up at him and wished she hadn't. All the fluttering in her stomach ceased, only to be replaced by a pounding pulse.

His eyes held that faraway look he sometimes got during

conversations, but when he glanced at her, they grew alert, then wary. "You need help with the lock?" He held out a key chain and removed a small key. A duplicate remained on the ring. "You can keep this, but you're welcome to remove the lock and leave it in the milk room."

Before she could thank him, he dove back into his hidey-hole. Though she hadn't wanted to see him, part of her had hoped he'd accompany her to the milk shed. Why was she disappointed about not spending time with someone who'd put her at the bottom of his list? And if she didn't stop bugging him, she might end up off that list altogether.

Katie trudged to the milk shed door and unlocked it. The last time she'd been in here, she'd been giddy with excitement, both about realizing she'd be getting milk and about being so close to Elam. Now it was as if they'd never been friends. She supposed they hadn't. She'd only assumed they had been.

Shaking off her disappointment, she dragged the hose toward the tank. Opening the outer cover, she unscrewed the cap. She carefully attached her hose, and then went outside to start the propane motor. Daed had filled it that morning, and she was overjoyed when the pump began to work. That meant she'd hooked everything up correctly.

Katie smiled. She hadn't needed Elam's help after all.

Except no milk flowed through the hose. She shut off the motor and ran into the milk shed. She'd been expecting a puddle of milk on the floor from faulty connections, but the floor was dry. She checked all the hookups again.

Then she stood. No milk flowing through the hose could only mean one thing. She stalked over to the bulk tank and pulled up the measuring stick Elam had shown her. The tank was empty.

A knock startled Elam from the depth of his concentration. He gripped the edges of the desk, trying to tamp down his rising irritation. *Not again.* He blew out a breath. He'd reached a tricky spot and had just worked out the problem. All he had to do was get it down before he forgot it.

"I asked if you needed help earlier," he called through the door.

She rattled the knob, and he shot out of his chair and raced to the door to prevent her from opening it. If she saw what he was doing. . .

Luckily, she stopped trying to enter, but she yelled, "I can't believe you'd do this to your goats!"

His goats? What was happening to his goats?

He slipped out of the office, trying to hide his work behind him. He quickly slammed the door shut. Katie stood only a few feet away, her hands on her hips, her face filled with fury. "You're so busy with whatever you're doing in that room"—she waved a hand toward his office door—"you're neglecting your goats."

Elam scanned the pens. His goats all appeared to be fine.

Katie gulped in a breath and continued, "What's so important in there that you'd rather be in there than talking to people or taking responsibility for helpless animals?"

"What are you talking about?" Her tirade had shattered the trancelike state he'd been in while he was working, but her words still made no sense.

"Your goats!" His indifference made her even more upset. "Do you have any idea how painful it is for goats when they aren't milked on time? It's already close to lunchtime."

"Maybe you should go have a bite of lunch yourself and calm down. Then we might be able to talk sensibly." Elam wasn't sure if he could talk sensibly even if she did calm down. Being near her had set his pulse racing so fast he wondered if he might have a heart attack.

"Calm down?" Her voice edged almost to hysteria. Then she pinched her lips into a straight line. "I have a better idea. Why don't you go back into your *office*"—she spat out the word—"and I'll take care of the goats?" She marched past him toward the milking machine. "Did you at least feed them today?"

"Of course I fed them."

"That's a relief. At least the poor things aren't starving."

"Wait," he said. "What are you doing?"

Katie headed toward the first goat. "Milking your goats."

What was wrong with her? Nobody milked goats in the middle of the day. He strode toward her and stopped her. "Thank you, but they've already been milked today."

Her jaw went slack. "They have?"

"I always milk them first thing every morning."

Her face flooded with gorgeous color. When her gaze met his, her eyes widened, and then she dropped her gaze. He swallowed hard and focused on the nearest goat.

"I'm sorry. I thought they hadn't been milked." She drew her brows together in a puzzled frown. "But then . . ."

"Then what?" Elam wished he could figure out why she'd been ranting.

Her eyes were teary, and her voice shook. "You sold my milk to Ray again. Why didn't you tell me? I know you don't like me, but I thought you'd honor your pledge."

"Katie, I wouldn't break a promise." He might tell a huge lie out of embarrassment—one she'd never forgive him for—but he'd never go back on his word.

She stared at the floor and shuffled one foot on the cement. "I didn't think so. That's why I assumed the goats hadn't been milked."

"I'm completely confused. You burst in here and accused me of not caring for my goats. Now you're saying I break my agreements."

He took a deep breath. "Your anger at me is totally justified. I deserve it. The things I said were terrible. And I totally understand you not wanting to forgive me, but—"

"That's not true," she burst out. "I did forgive you."

"Oh." He stood there in shock for moment. "You did? I assumed when you didn't answer my note—"

"What note?"

"The one I left taped to the milk can on Tuesday."

"I never got a note."

She hadn't received his note, but she'd forgiven him? Elam's heart soared, but she'd been avoiding him. "I spent hours writing notes to you, trying to find the right way to apologize."

Her eyes bored into him. "What did it say?"

"I don't remember," he muttered. "I apologized for lying when I said you were at the bottom of the list." Things like this were easier to write than to put into conversation.

Katie lowered herself onto a nearby milking stool. "I'm not at the bottom?" She whispered as if she couldn't believe it.

"Of course not."

"I see. I'm second to the bottom then."

She looked so crestfallen he wanted to hold her in his arms to comfort her. *Whoa, Elam!* Where did that thought come from?

"When I said I lied, I meant it was a big lie, a huge one."

The corners of her lips edged up a little. "A really huge one?"

He nodded, but hoped she wouldn't ask what number. "I was embarrassed and wanted them to stop teasing me. I said the first thing I could think of." He stared down at the floor. "I never thought you'd hear it."

"I guess, in a way, that was my fault."

Startled, he stared at her.

"Didn't I tell you to blurt out the first thing that came to mind in conversation instead of evaluating it?" She gave a short chuckle.

"I'm glad you can laugh about it." Then he sobered. "I do want you to know I confessed to everyone at the table that I lied."

"You did? And did you tell them what number I really am?"

"No, I learned my lesson. From now on, I'll always think before I speak."

Katie twisted her mouth into an exaggerated pout. "That's no fun. Why don't you think about it and tell me?"

He'd been dreading that question. No way could he admit the truth. "I'm still thinking."

"Elam!" Mose yelled so loudly they both jumped. "Where are you?"

As he shuffled into the barn, she jumped to her feet, but it put her too close to Elam. He stepped back and so did she.

His Daed's eyebrows rose. "What's going on in here?" He frowned at Elam, and his eyes flashed a warning that he planned to give him a lecture.

"Katie came into the barn to . . ." Why had she come in? They'd gotten sidetracked.

"Because there's no milk in the bulk tank," she supplied.

Elam and his Daed both gaped at her.

"No milk?" Elam echoed. "Are you sure you hooked everything up right?"

His Daed eyed him. Yes, they'd been in here a long time for Elam not to have asked that question.

"Why don't we go have a look?"

When they reached the empty milk tank, he and his Daed said at the same time, "Ray Gifford."

"Katie, I'm so sorry." Elam tried to convey an apology with his eyes. "It won't happen ever again. If I have to sit here every morning to prevent Ray from stealing the milk again, I will."

"Why not change the lock and give Katie the new key?" his Daed suggested.

Elam reddened. That would have been a sensible solution. This blurting things out always seemed to make a fool of him.

She giggled. "It's nice of you to offer."

"I'll wait for him tomorrow morning, though, just to make sure he understands." And that he didn't try to pry off the lock.

"Well, if there's no milk, I should be going." She headed toward her wagon.

"I'm so sorry, Katie." He hoped she understood he meant more than just the milk theft.

Her soft, "I know," reassured him she did.

12

Clouds covered the moon and dawn had not yet broken when Elam sat outside in the darkness, waiting for Ray. Although he worried about his deadline and getting the goats milked on time, Ray usually arrived about this time of the morning. Elam had taken his Daed's advice and purchased a new lock, but he wanted to be sure Ray understood all the milk on this farm belonged to Katie, at least until she didn't need it anymore.

Elam still smarted from his Daed's lecture the night before. Actually, his Daed's words stung less than the thought that, once again, he'd done something to damage Katie's reputation. Elam had no idea how long they'd been in the barn together, but it was definitely long enough to raise the neighbors' eyebrows if someone had noticed. As his Daed reminded him, with everyone believing the two of them were courting, people were keeping a closer eye on them.

Elam agreed he should do whatever he could to protect her from gossip, but for some reason, whenever the two of them started talking, he lost all track of time. The only solution was not to talk to her. Or only have conversations with someone else present. Neither of those options appealed to him.

When Ray's tanker coasted into the back lane, Elam waited for Ray to get out, then rose. Ray hummed as he headed toward the door. Evidently, he hadn't seen Elam. Not wanting to startle him, Elam edged into the circle of light cast by Ray's taillights.

Ray jumped and clutched his chest. "You trying to give me a heart attack?" he snarled.

Elam had expected an angry response to his request, but he hadn't intended to rile Ray before they even spoke. "I'm sorry. It's so dark out here. I wanted to be sure you saw me."

"Oh, I did all right." His face, shaded red from the taillights' beam, took on a glare of defiance.

"Listen," Elam said, "I just wanted to be sure there's no misunderstanding. Our contract ended on Wednesday. All the milk belongs to someone else now."

"Nope." Ray grinned. "We're month-to-month, and I was here yesterday, so I got the rest of the month."

"Sorry, but I told you last week that the supply ended on Wednesday. You got an extra day free. I won't charge you for it, but I've changed the lock."

"You dirty rotten—"

Elam held up a hand. "Look, Ray, I don't want trouble." He spoke calmly. "I understand you need a larger supply, so Daed and I put together a list of goat farms that are willing to sell you milk." He held out the paper. "They're a little distance from here, but I hope enough of them will make it worth your while."

Grumbling under his breath, Ray stuffed the paper into his pocket without glancing at it. "Doesn't mean I still don't plan to get access to your milk. You owe me."

"No, Ray. I let you finish out the month and gave you an extra day free."

Ray wheeled around and stomped to his tanker. Just before he slammed the door, he growled, "If these don't work out, I'll be back."

Two of Elam's second cousins who lived about twenty miles away had agreed to sell to Ray. Several others said they'd consider it. It would mean a longer drive for him, but with several goat farmers in the same area, traveling that distance would be worth his while. Elam bowed his head and prayed Ray would be richly blessed with all the milk he needed for his company. And Elam thanked God for saving the milk supply for Katie.

Katie climbed into the wagon with a joyful heart. Elam had promised to have milk for her today. That was good news, especially since she'd lost yesterday's supply. She did extra baking to make more money, and yesterday's sales had been enough to pay off the farrier and two of the smaller bills.

All of those blessings made her sing hymns of praise. For her, though, the greatest blessing was a restored relationship with Elam. Knowing she was on his friend list thrilled her, and having a chance to talk to him yesterday had been wunderbar.

Today she'd respect his privacy and his rules. No more knocking on the door and disturbing him at his work. She still remained curious, wondering what he did behind closed doors to make the strange sounds. And why was he so secretive about it?

This time when she reached the Hertzlers' driveway, both Mose and Elam waited for her. Her stomach clenched. Did they have bad news? Why else would they be waiting?

But as she walked toward them, Elam held out a small key. "You should find last night's and this morning's milk in there. And, yes, I remembered to milk the goats."

Katie's cheeks heated. "Ach, I'm so sorry. I never should have spoken out of turn like that."

"Neither should I."

Elam still seemed a bit chagrined, and Katie hastened to assure him, "I told you I forgave you. So let's put it behind us."

He grinned. "And I've forgiven you for yesterday, so let's start fresh."

Mose cleared his throat. Katie had been so caught up in her conversation with Elam, she'd forgotten he was there.

"*Gute mariye*, Mose. It's so nice to see you." Katie flashed him a smile.

"Jah, *vell*, I suppose you're wondering what I'm doing here."

She scrunched her eyebrows in confusion. "You live here."

Mose laughed. "True enough. But I meant why I'm here overseeing—"

Elam interrupted. "Daed, I don't think we need to get into that. I'm sure Katie is eager to get her milk and be on her way. She has a lot of soap to make, and did you know she does plenty of baking for her sisters to sell at the farm market?" His rush of words seemed to be preventing his Daed from finishing his sentence. "I need to get back to work. I only wanted to make sure Katie had the correct key. Now that I know she does, we can let her pump the milk."

Katie had never seen Elam so talkative. It made her curious about what he hoped to keep his Daed from saying. But she didn't want to add to his discomfort, so she bid them both goodbye and walked off with her key.

Behind her, Elam said, "Daed, please, we don't need to bother Katie with that."

"Son, I think she should know."

She moved out of hearing range, so she had no idea what Mose wanted to tell her and Elam did not. One other small mystery to add to her to-be-solved list. Elam's work was probably something deadly dull and uninteresting. Maybe he fixed dented pans. The sound reminded her of tapping the ball peen hammer on the pie tins. She'd heard leatherworkers before, but those sounds were much louder and sharper, not as close together.

Katie pushed aside her musings to concentrate on hooking up the pump correctly. When everything was ready, she went over to the tank and lifted the measuring stick. She smiled. Almost a full tank, just as Elam had promised. She went outside to switch on the propane motor. A few seconds later, milk gurgled through the hose.

Thank you, Lord!

When the tank had filled, she made sure everything was back in place, then rinsed out the tank and hosed down the floor. Before she hopped in the wagon, she noticed Elam and his Daed still in earnest conversation. She didn't want to interrupt, but she was so thrilled about her first successful pumping, she hurried over to thank them.

Elam's smile was tense, but his eyes held a warm welcome. "Everything all right?"

"More than all right," Katie enthused. "It's wonderful. This will be so much easier and save so much time compared to hauling milk cans." She turned to Mose. "Not that I'm not grateful for the cans. They were a huge help."

Elam laughed. "So I take it your first experience with pumping went well."

"Definitely. I did have a question about your goats. Do you freshen them all at once or at different times? It would help me to gauge how much milk I'll be getting."

Mose's bushy white eyebrows arched. "You sound like you know something about tending goats."

"I have four of my own."

"So what would you do if you were planning the freshening?" Mose leaned forward as if intensely interested in her answer.

Was he testing her to see if she'd answer correctly?

"If they were my goats, I'd stagger it. That way the milk supply would be more consistent throughout the year." Katie hoped that was the best answer. "But everyone's different."

Mose chuckled and elbowed Elam. "Did you hear that, son? She sounds like she'd make a good goat farmer. Maybe Katie could help out here so you'd have more time in that office of yours."

A pained expression crossed Elam's face. "I always take care of the goats before I do my other work."

"Jah, work that you refuse to discuss."

Katie couldn't believe it. His own father had no idea what Elam did in the office? That made her even more curious than she already was.

"It pays the bills when goat milk doesn't." Elam's tight-lipped reply made it clear his Daed had hurt his feelings.

Katie wanted to smooth things over between them, but Mose said to her, "I agree with you on staggering the freshening. Is that what you do with your own goats?"

Katie nibbled on her lower lip. "If I had more, I would. I don't have a buck, so it makes it that much more difficult." She'd have to come up with money soon, though, or they'd have no more milk.

"You're welcome to use one of our bucks to freshen your goats," Mose said.

"Thank you for your offer, but money is tight now. I will keep it in mind for the future."

"Would you consider an exchange? Time with a buck and a reduced rate on the milk for helping Elam with the freshening? My arthritis makes it harder for me to assist, and I'm sure Elam would appreciate the chance to have additional time in his office."

Katie would be happy to help both of them. And it would mean more time around goats, which she loved, and more time around Elam, which she—maybe she'd better not finish that thought. Anyway, in exchange for two things she definitely needed? What else could she say but an emphatic "jah"?

"Daed, did you forget why you're out here?"

Mose flapped a hand. "I just nabbed me a goat expert. That should make you happy. You can hide out in your office more often." The twinkle in his eyes made it clear he was teasing.

Elam merely shook his head at his father. Katie hoped she hadn't stepped into a disagreement between Elam and his Daed.

The minute Katie drove out of the driveway, Elam confronted his Daed. "What were you thinking? We can't have Katie here helping with the goats."

His Daed only smiled. "I couldn't have found a more perfect match."

"This needs to stop. Katie has a boyfriend, and I—" Elam couldn't finish that sentence or his Daed would crow and strut around like a rooster. Elam had only recently realized he was in love with Katie. That was hard enough to deal with when he'd decided never to marry. And if she were around all the time, how would he ever get any work done? Just knowing she was outside his door, even if he were locked inside, would be torture.

His Daed tapped his foot on the ground, waiting for Elam to finish the sentence he'd started.

"Well, I couldn't get any work done with Katie here," he finished lamely. "With anyone here," he added to be sure his Daed didn't misinterpret his meaning. "Besides, with me in the office and Katie in the barn, won't people get the wrong impression? What about that hour-long lecture you gave me last night about protecting Katie's reputation?"

"For your information, son, when I said *match*, I meant a good fit for goat care, but I'm interested in the fact that you jumped to a different conclusion."

"Daed, I want an honest answer. Goats aside, are you playing matchmaker?"

His Daed stroked his beard and refused to meet Elam's eyes.

"I'll take that as a jah. Please don't do this, Daed," Elam begged. "Someone could end up hurt."

The more Katie thought about Mose's offer, the more concerned she became. She already had more work than she could handle at home. And with the soap orders, she'd added a nearly impossible workload to her already full days. But she had no way to pay for breeding, so Mose's offer came as an answer to prayer. It also meant more time around Elam, which she would enjoy, but how much time could she spend around him without giving away her true feelings?

She argued with herself while she baked and made soap. By dinnertime, she'd come to no conclusions. She'd already told Mose jah, but if her Daed forbade it, Mose would understand. Daed might object to her spending time on another farm, when so many chores needed doing here at home.

Her sisters arrived home before dinner, and Leah came into the kitchen to help prepare the meal. She glanced around to see if anyone else was in the kitchen before leaning close to Katie. "I overheard people talking about you today. They're saying you and Elam are courting."

"Whatever gave them that idea?"

"He was here for long visits most days last week, and then you went to his house."

Katie chopped the end of the ham into small chunks. "I hope you corrected them and explained about the milk deliveries."

"I tried, but they just rolled their eyes. They said the visits were too long for deliveries." Leah added green beans to the pot with the ham, while Katie sautéed onions.

Katie sighed. Didn't people have anything better to do than to watch other people's driveways? "I hope Elam hasn't heard that gossip."

"I expect he has," Leah said. "According to most people, his Daed was the one who started the rumors."

Elam had warned his Daed against that, but it seemed Mose hadn't listened.

After their silent prayer at the dinner table, Katie described Mose's offer to her Daed. She didn't mention she'd be working with Elam.

Daed frowned in thought. "It sounds like a good opportunity, and I know how much you love goats. You could learn a lot from an experienced goat farmer like Mose."

Leah smiled. "You've always said you'd like to be a goat farmer someday. Here's your chance."

After stabbing several green beans, Daed stopped with the fork halfway to his mouth. "I do have some concerns, Dochter."

Katie sat, tense and waiting, while he chewed. She could guess one of his concerns. Especially if he'd heard the same rumors Leah had.

"First of all, the chores. You do all the cooking, most of the cleaning, and the majority of the baking. In addition, you've added this large soap order." Daed set his fork on his plate. "When will you find the time to go to Mose's farm?"

"I did worry about that."

He nodded and chewed another bite of the ham-and-green-bean

casserole. "The boys and I can take over the goat milking. The summer market hours will dwindle as harvest ends, so your sisters will have more time."

"Lizzie and the boys will be heading back to school in a few weeks, though." Katie slid her food around on her plate. She'd have to clean it off soon—their Amish ways did not allow for wasting food—but right now she was too nervous to eat.

"I'll have more days at home starting in September," Leah said. "I can take over the cooking and baking on those days. And we won't need to make as many baked goods."

"We've all been helping with the soapmaking at night," Lizzie pointed out.

Katie smiled at her and the boys. "Jah, that's been a *gut* help."

"Lizzie can make meals after school and on Saturday when Leah's at the market. And there'll be time for some chores before school." Daed had divided up almost all of Katie's duties.

"Then what will I do?" she asked.

"Work at the goat farm and make soap."

13

Once school started and Leah worked fewer days, Daed insisted everyone begin the new chore schedule. With more free time on her hands, Katie let Mose know she could start working two days a week. After the harvest, she'd extend it to three days.

Mose's delighted smile warmed her heart. "That will be perfect."

"What do you want me to do first?" she asked.

"I see Elam hasn't mucked out the goat pens. If you could do that, I'd appreciate it." He grimaced and rubbed at his back.

"Are you all right?"

"Fine, fine."

But he didn't look fine. He appeared to be in pain.

"I've mucked out plenty of goat pens. Why don't you go in the house and lie down?"

He argued, but Katie won and convinced him to rest. After Mose limped off, she tried to find a rake or scoop for cleaning. She walked through the whole barn, opening cupboard doors, peering in corners, and checking for hanging pegs. The tools had to be somewhere.

Neither of the two people who could answer her question were available. One was in the house lying down. The other was tapping away in the office nearby. The noise stopped. Maybe Elam was taking a break. Surely he wouldn't mind answering a quick question when he wasn't busy.

Katie went to the door and knocked. Elam muttered something, but she couldn't make out the words. She wasn't positive, but he might have said, "Come in." Eager to get started on the job, she opened the door.

Elam was running his hands through his hair and looking distraught. When he caught sight of her, his eyes widened and his mouth dropped open. "What are you doing?" he croaked.

Shelves of books lined the walls of the room. That was no surprise. He'd always loved to read. In the center of the desk was the tool that made the clicking sound—a typewriter. But what was on the desk shocked her so much she stopped dead. She forgot why she'd come in.

What in the world were those doing on his desk?

He tried to hide them with his sleeve, but she'd know them anywhere.

"Emily Fox? You read those?" Filled with disbelief, Katie pointed to the novels. Then her face heated. She'd just admitted she was familiar with the books.

The bishop had forbidden them from indulging in such worldly stories, so Elam might wonder how she knew who Emily Fox was.

He was staring at her with such consternation she had to say something. "Some of my friends and I read them in secret. I know we shouldn't, but those novels are the only ones that are true to the Amish lifestyle. We all like them. The girls who work at the market take turns buying a new one every once in a while, and we all pass them around."

He still hadn't responded, so she asked again, "So do you read Emily Fox?"

He hesitated. "I've never opened these."

"How could anyone not open an Emily Fox novel? They're filled with adventure and—" She stopped just before she said *romance*. She didn't want to tell him, but they had the best love stories she'd ever read. Not that she'd read many. "I can hardly wait for the next one."

She gestured toward the one closest to his hand. "In that one, the heroine is trapped in a barn fire. The hero saves her when she jumps from the barn loft window. It's so exciting! Oh, I hope I didn't spoil it for you."

"No you didn't."

Had he said that sarcastically? She couldn't be sure. "So you don't intend to read them?"

"I have no desire to crack open the covers." Elam's face was pinched up, but Katie couldn't tell if he was embarrassed to be caught with the books, or if something else was bothering him.

How ridiculous to have the books if he wasn't going to read them. "Then why do you have them?" Even as she asked, it dawned on her. A typewriter. A small stack of paper by his hand. "You're writing a book?"

He didn't respond, but he looked sick.

She started around the desk to peek at what he'd been typing, but he rolled the sheet of paper out of the typewriter and set it facedown on top of the other pages, then set his hand on top of them to hold them down.

The way he held them, so determined not to let her peek, appeared suspicious. And from that, she concluded, "You're copying her books. Plagiarizing them."

He didn't meet her eyes, only stared down at the papers under his hand, a guilty expression on his face.

"You hide out in this office every day, typing, instead of tending your goats, which I'm going to do for you? And you're busy copying someone else's book?"

"I am not copying anyone else's books."

Then why was he so determined not to let her see what he was writing? "So why didn't you want me to see it?" Then a thought struck her. Her cheeks hot, she asked, "What you're writing isn't bad, is it?"

"No, I wouldn't write anything like that. And I don't like anyone to see my writing while I'm doing it. Not even Virginia."

"That's the Englisher who was here? Is she going to publish your book?"

"She's an agent, but she'll take the book to a publisher."

"Do you think she'll be able to sell it?"

He made a strange choking sound. "I hope so."

Elam sat there frozen, as Katie unleashed a whirlwind around him. He had no idea what to say, what to admit, what to explain. He hadn't expected her to barge in, so he had no time to hide the books or the evidence. Now he was tongue-tied.

She seemed convinced he read Emily Fox, which was bad enough, but what would she think if she knew the truth? And she assumed this was his first book.

When Katie had pointed to the typewriter and to the sheets of paper stacked up on his desk and accused him of being a writer, Elam's stomach had churned. At least he'd had the presence of mind to take that sheet of paper from the typewriter. If the bishop ever found out . . .

With her being a talker, who knew how far she'd spread this? His carefully guarded secret might be exposed to everyone. He had to find a way to stop her from leaking this information.

He held up a hand to stop her questioning. "Katie, I asked you never to come in the office. I intended to keep this private. If other people find out, especially the bishop, I'd have to give up work I love. This job helps support the goat farm because it's not profitable on its own."

"So you're really a writer?" When he nodded, she asked, "And when you say you don't want anyone to know, do you mean not even your Daed?"

"That's right. I know I'm asking a lot. I don't want you to lie for me, but—"

"I understand. When I walk out of this office and close the door, I'll shut my lips. Your secret is safe with me."

"Thank you, Katie. You don't know what that means to me."

"You helped me when I needed it. If you hadn't collected that goat milk for a week or agreed to sell me your milk, we'd have lost the farm. Keeping quiet is one small way to repay you."

"You don't owe me anything, but I'm grateful for your silence."

After she left the room, he buried his head in his hands. More than anything, he wanted to trust her, but could he? Or had his writing life come to an end?

Still stunned by Elam's revelation, Katie walked back into the barn in a daze. She'd been eager to discover his secret, but now that she had, she was sorry she'd barged into the office. Carrying the weight of someone else's secret was a heavy burden.

She started back to the goat pens and realized that she'd never asked him where to find the tools. Much as she hated to disturb him again, she had to do some work before Mose returned. Crossing the floor, she returned to the office door. He hadn't started tapping—typing—again, so she knocked.

"Elam, I won't come in. I just have a quick question. Where do you keep the tools for mucking out the pens?"

"The fine-tooth rake is right by the barn door. And the dustpan, broom, and slotted scoop are all nearby. Use whatever you prefer."

"Danke," she called through the door.

How could she have missed them? She headed toward the door and quickly discovered how she'd missed them: They weren't there.

She couldn't bother him a second time. He'd already started typing. Yet she didn't want to disturb Mose if he was lying down. She stood there uncertainly trying to decide who to ask, when Mose shuffled into the barn, his hands filled with tools.

"I thought you might need these." He held them out. "I washed them earlier and left them out to dry."

She studied his face. Like his son, he seemed to be hiding something. Who washed their mucking tools? That seemed highly suspicious. Had he set her up, hoping she'd ask for Elam's help? After what Leah had said, Katie had no doubt he'd been ignoring Elam's plea to stop matchmaking.

When Katie left, Elam resolved to install a knob with a lock on his office door the next day. If he'd done that before, Katie couldn't have barged in on him. He wasn't about to take a chance of it happening again. Not with her. Not with anyone.

She'd only discovered part of his secret. He didn't want anyone to find out the rest.

14

That night as they made soap, Katie realized she'd been too busy to answer Jonas's letter. She wasn't sure what to say. Should she ask him what his future plans were? At this point, he probably didn't know. Where did that leave their relationship?

She'd also been procrastinating because her attraction to Elam made it harder to write. Although she and Elam enjoyed each other's company, she had no idea if he would ever marry anyone, let alone her. And his secret concerned her. She had a feeling he'd been holding something back about his secret writing, but she couldn't figure out what it could be.

Now that she knew, would he be more open about letting her in the office? Maybe he'd even show her what he was working on? Actually, she'd thought her curiosity would be satisfied if she peeked inside, but now she had a burning desire to read what he had written.

She should have asked what kind of stories he wrote. If Emily Fox served as his inspiration, maybe they'd be romances. He did say he hadn't read her books, though. Why, then, were they on his desk? Unless he planned to read them but hadn't started yet. He may have been embarrassed to tell her that.

"Katie," Leah said, "isn't that batch ready yet? We should get these in the shed soon. It's getting dark."

Jerking herself back to the kitchen, Katie checked Aaron's stirring. She'd been miles away in her thoughts, but over the past weeks, she'd made so many batches, she automatically followed all the steps.

"I'll get the molds ready," she told Aaron. When she returned, she helped him pour the soap into the molds.

Later, on the way to the shed, she checked on Buttermilk. Daed had moved the goat house and climbing ramps farther away from the fencing. Perhaps that would keep the lively goat from escaping.

That night as she fell into bed, exhausted, her thoughts returned to Elam rather than Jonas, but she vowed to write a return letter in the morning before heading off to the goat farm.

In the dreamland between sleeping and waking, Katie woke with a start to crashing and banging. She'd overslept, and her sisters were loading the van. After dressing hurriedly, she ran downstairs to help them.

After everyone had left for the day, Katie forced herself to sit at the kitchen table to write a brief letter to Jonas. Guilt plagued her over her excitement at seeing Elam that morning, so her missive was brief, unlike her previous letters. Instead of her usual greeting of *Dear Jonas*, she opted for a quick, scrawled note:

Jonas,

I'm rushing out the door to work at a goat farm. Life has been busy here. I received a huge order for soaps, so the whole family is working long hours to make them. I'm sorry I won't have much time to write until the order is finished in November.

You sounded excited about your news. I'll be praying for you.

Sincerely,

Katie

Somehow, she couldn't bring herself to write *Love, Katie. Sincerely* sounded a bit stilted and businesslike, and she hoped he didn't think her coldness resulted from his racing announcement.

Glad to have that obligation over, she slid the letter into an envelope, placed the stamp on it, and headed out to hitch up the wagon. Since when had writing to Jonas seemed like a chore instead of a joy? She wished the answer wasn't Elam, but she had to admit her spirits always lifted whenever she saw him.

She stopped her horse at the end of the driveway to slide the letter into the mailbox and raise the flag. Was it wrong of her to hope Jonas would take a long time to respond?

She put her worries about Jonas and their relationship from her mind while the horse trotted down the now-familiar country lanes leading to Elam's. She hummed tunes and sometimes burst out in song while she enjoyed the beautiful scenery—cornfields towering by the sides of the road, women and children picking vegetables in gardens bursting with rows of green leaves, and horses pulling combines. Ordinary scenes of daily life filled her with elation, or perhaps the excitement was related to her final destination.

When Katie entered the barn, Elam's office door was closed as usual, and steady clicking occurred inside. But the door sported a shiny new doorknob, one with a hole for a key. The happiness she'd experienced on the way over took a nosedive. The locked door made it clear he wanted her to stay out of his life. He was guarding his privacy. From her.

Mose hadn't appeared to greet her, so she picked up the rake, which she found in its usual place, and let herself into a pen. Her mind drifted as she worked, raking carefully. She allowed herself to daydream that last night's dream was real. She had dreamed of Elam. He held her close, her cheek pressed against his chest, the steady thump of his heart comforting in her ear. She floated far above her earthly work and enjoyed the heavenly sensations.

The click of a door opening barely registered until Elam spoke. "I've never seen anyone so rapturous while mucking out stalls."

She thudded back to reality and turned startled eyes in his direction. Heat flooded up her neck and splashed across her face. "I try to think of other things when I work," she managed to stammer out and hoped he wouldn't ask what she'd been thinking.

"I'll have to experiment with that, although I do often plot as I work."

"I see you got a lock for your door." *Great, Katie. Blurt out the first thing that comes to mind.* She needed lessons from Elam in using discretion and thinking before speaking. Maybe that's why God had brought her here to the Hertzlers' farm. She could help him overcome his shyness, and he could teach her to guard her tongue.

He shuffled his feet. "I had been thinking about it for a while." He rubbed the back of his neck. "Yesterday provided the impetus to get it done." His face reddened. "Not that I did it to lock you out. I mean, I was going to do it anyway so no one else could walk in there. The next person might not be as understanding."

So he said. But who else would barge into his office? Ray had gotten the milk outside. Elam's Daed respected his privacy. If he'd been worried about Virginia, he would have installed a lock before her visit. In fact, he'd said he didn't like her looking over his shoulder, which meant she must have tried. So she'd been in the office. The only person he needed to lock out was Katie.

"I didn't mean to interrupt your happy thoughts. I needed to run into the house for a book."

"A book? But you have shelves of them in your office."

He winced, reminding her that he hadn't appreciated her intruding. "That office is small, so I can't keep everything I use out there. Only the most important books."

"I see." She wondered if he had rooms filled with books inside the house too.

After he left, Katie returned to the mucking, but her joy had leaked out as reality returned. He had reinforced the fact that the lock's message was, *Keep out, Katie Kurtz.*

Elam hurried across the driveway to the kitchen door, hoping Katie hadn't seen through his flimsy excuse. He'd mainly wanted a chance to talk to her, to see her. The book could have waited. He could have checked it tonight because he wouldn't be ready to work on that scene until later this week.

He dawdled going upstairs so it didn't appear he was rushing back, even though that was all he wanted to do. He'd stood, enchanted by that rapturous smile on her face while she did a filthy job. He couldn't help contrasting her work ethic with Virginia's squeamishness.

Katie did what needed to be done. He'd never seen such a hard worker. He'd been amazed at her kitchen counters filled with breads and pies, and her willingness to add a huge soap order to her daily chores. Somehow, she managed to squeeze in time to help with their goats, and at the end of the day she pumped milk to take home. She must work late into the night to turn that all into soap. Yet, through it all, she stayed unruffled, smiling, and good-natured. She'd make a wonderful *gut* wife.

Elam stopped himself. There was a time when the word *wife* would have given him hives. Now it brought only a pang of sadness. She had brought about that change. In her, he'd found his ideal match. Where else could he find a hardworking wife who loved goat farming and lived her faith? Open and honest, she'd set about teaching him how to communicate in spoken words.

His lips curved into a smile. Best of all, she was passionate about Emily Fox books. They'd bonded over their secret love of fiction. Not all Amish girls would admit that they read Amish romances, but Katie had been up-front about it. Seeing her face light up as she described the plot of *The Firefighter's Rescue* had delighted him.

She might be the perfect match—Daed would be gloating if he knew—but there was a major obstacle in that she belonged to someone else.

Elam checked the fact he needed to, then searched through the bookshelves for a research book that would seem suitably scholarly. He couldn't bring the other book with him, or she might guess his secret. She'd already discovered more about him than anyone else knew, including his Daed. He suspected she wouldn't be as accepting of the rest of his secret.

Carrying a thesaurus, Elam returned to the barn. He slowed before entering to enjoy her snatches of song. She'd likely be too self-conscious to continue once he entered. What would it be like to have her around every day for the rest of his life?

"You all right, son?" His Daed's voice boomed through the kitchen window.

Of course Daed had seen him standing here, mooning over Katie. He was probably congratulating himself on the success of his plan.

"I'm fine, Daed."

His Daed's voice stopped Katie's singing, and now that she knew Elam was out here, he had to walk into the barn. He struggled to appear nonchalant as he strode inside, but he paused to admire the goat pens filled with fresh bedding, which should have been his job.

Metal clanged beside him. She was inches away, returning the rake to its usual spot. His mouth went dry. He'd been so busy staring at the goat pens, he hadn't registered her within touching distance. He grasped his suspenders to keep from reaching out when she blinked and glanced into his eyes. His heart stopped as he focused on her lips, slightly parted in surprise, then it thundered in his ears, so loudly he worried she could hear its beat.

The dreamy expression had returned to her eyes, the one she'd had earlier before he'd disturbed her. He often went into a trance like that when he was in the writing zone, but he wasn't writing, and she wasn't a character on the page. She was real and so close he could encircle her with his arms.

The edges of his suspenders bit into his hand as he struggled to control that desire. He had to break free, to move away before he did something he'd regret. He took one step backward. Then two, but each one was like pulling on hardening taffy, almost impossible. He'd made it three steps when disappointment flashed in her eyes. Had she been yearning for his touch as much as he had yearned to touch her?

"I-I'd better get back to work." He was astonished he could speak a coherent sentence. "The pens look nice. Clean, I mean." Now he was babbling. He had to go before he made even more of a fool of himself. Tearing his gaze from her face, he spun around.

"Wait!" She sounded almost as desperate as he felt.

He turned, but wished he hadn't. She drew him like a magnet. He planted his feet so he wouldn't move closer.

She appeared as startled as he was by her request. She hesitated and stared at him, seemingly at a loss for words. After a few seconds, she said, "I just wanted to know what else you need me to do."

"Maybe you'd better ask my Daed."

"Jah, of course."

She looked so downcast, he almost returned to her. Her gaze wandered to the doorknob.

Had he hurt her feelings by installing that lock? He hadn't meant it to shut her out. Or maybe he had. She'd gotten too close for comfort.

Katie couldn't face Mose right now. Not after she'd been locking gazes with his son. The elderly man was much too perceptive. Rubbing the fabric of her work apron through her fingers, she tried to rein in her runaway heart. All she'd wanted was for Elam to wrap his arms around her, holding her close the way he had in her dreams.

For a few moments, it had seemed as if her dreams were about to come true. Then he'd shuttered his eyes and stepped back. Each step had been an ever-widening rift between them. It had been folly to call him back. She'd almost begged him to stay, but she'd caught herself in time. She only hoped her expression hadn't revealed the truth.

15

Katie knocked at the back door, and Mose called through the screen for her to come in. The farmhouse kitchen, which may have once been homey, now had faded paint, scarred linoleum, and a huge pile of dishes in the sink.

"Ignore the dishes." Mose had his legs stretched out in front of him with a hot water bottle on one. "I'll get to them later. Or Elam will wash them tonight."

She could never let dishes sit in the sink. "Why don't I do them?"

"No need." Mose struggled to get up.

She motioned for him to stay where he was. "It won't take long, and while I work, you can tell me what you want me to do next with the goats. Should I brush them?"

He chuckled. "They'd love that, but not today. The dishes will be enough." He passed a hand over his eyes and rubbed at his forehead. "For a minute there, you reminded me of Martha. She used to stand there washing stacks of dishes when we had our *youngie* at home."

Katie gave him a sympathetic smile.

"I miss her every day. When you have a good marriage, it's hard to say goodbye to a spouse."

"I can imagine it is." She filled the sink with soapy water and laid a clean towel on the counter.

"Choose wisely. That's the best advice I can give. Make sure your husband honors God and loves others. If he does that, any other problems can be worked out."

She nodded. She was unsure if she'd ever need Mose's advice, but maybe she needed it more than she thought. Jonas's last letter came to mind. He'd been reluctant to kneel before the church and confess his faith. Would he ever choose God over worldly pursuits?

"But you didn't come here for marriage advice. About the goats— you've done enough for today, but I'd like to freshen the goats the next time you come. When will that be?"

She scrubbed at congealed food on one of the plates. "The market is closed on Monday and Wednesday."

"We'll plan for Monday then."

The door banged open, startling Katie.

Elam skidded to a stop in the doorway. What was Katie doing in their kitchen? Washing dishes, no less? Another job that should have been his.

He frowned at his father, who shrugged. Was this another one of his Daed's setups? Elam didn't need a demonstration that she was a good housewife. He'd seen her immaculate kitchen and tasted her baking.

"You shouldn't be doing those," he blurted out. "I'll take care of them."

"It's no trouble." Without looking up, she lifted a plate from the suds and scrubbed at dried-on eggs. "I'm almost done."

That was far from the truth. Most of those dishes needed to be soaked, which he'd been planning to do later this afternoon, after he finished the latest chapter.

She had not only taken over his barn chores, but now she was taking over his inside jobs. What would his Daed ask her to do next? Sweep the house? Do the laundry?

"Daed, Katie agreed to help with the goats. It's not fair to ask her to do our housework."

"He didn't ask me. I volunteered," she assured him. "Actually, I insisted." Her light, trilling laughter made him glance over at her.

Taking his attention from his Daed had been a mistake. Sunlight streaming in the window highlighted her auburn hair. Her head, bent over the plate, exposed the soft skin at the back of her neck. Elam stood mesmerized while she and his Daed talked.

He tore his gaze away when his Daed said, "Elam would be glad to pick up your goats in our trailer, wouldn't you, son?"

Lost in Katie's beauty and his fantasies of them eating together with her sitting beside him and favoring him with her radiant smile, Elam scrambled to catch up on the conversation. "Oh, um, of course." Whatever his Daed had just volunteered him for had better be something he wanted to do.

"That would be such a big help." She turned her grateful gaze in his direction, melting his heart. "If you really don't mind, that is."

He caught himself before he said he'd do anything for her, especially if it involved her gazing at him with those sparkling green eyes and her lips curving in that sweet smile "I don't mind."

"Are you sure? I have one goat who's pretty rambunctious."

"We have plenty of those." So now Elam had one clue. He'd discovered he'd volunteered to do something with her goats. Most likely freshening.

His Daed smiled at Katie. "I'd like to get started freshening soon after milking on Monday. Would it be too early if Elam picked up your goats before he starts?"

Second clue: I'll be picking up Katie's goats on Monday. Very early.

"That would be fine." She rinsed another dish and set it on the towel she'd laid on the counter. "On market day, my sisters leave at dawn, so we've made it a habit to rise that early every day."

"*Gut, gut.*" Daed eyed Elam, a half-smile playing across his face. "I'm sure you won't mind driving to Katie's before dawn."

Of course he wouldn't. He'd do anything for Katie.

Elam missed Katie's presence in the barn over the next few days. She only stopped by to pick up milk. He had trouble concentrating on his writing whenever she was around. He made excuses to go out and talk to her, or he watched her from the window.

On Sunday at church, his own community began congratulating him on courting her. This time he kept his mouth shut and didn't deny it. If he had any doubts as to where the rumors originated, they disappeared when he walked up behind Daed, talking to several other men waiting in line to fill their plates at the after-church meal.

"Yes, I'm thrilled he's courting Katie Kurtz. She's at our house a lot because I'm training her to be a goat farmer. She has goats of her own, so she's doing a wonderful *gut* job."

"Daed," Elam said warningly.

His Daed jumped, but faced him with a smile. "Isn't Katie doing well with the goats?"

"I don't know," Elam said firmly. "I don't see much of her. The goat pens are always spotless, so she must be good at mucking out."

His Daed's frown told him his answer hadn't been what he'd wanted.

After the previous Sunday's fiasco, perhaps Elam should have guarded his tongue, but it bothered him that people were linking his name with Katie's—something he wouldn't mind at all if she were free to date.

His cousin Miriam and her husband, Luke, had attended the

service today, and Elam could only guess why. During the meal, Luke sat beside Elam. He leaned close and whispered, "Miriam wants to talk to you. Can you meet her outside by the buggy before we leave?"

Elam had a good idea what Miriam's topic would be. And he was right. She waited impatiently for him as people began heading home.

The minute he arrived, Miriam asked. "So what's this I hear about you and Katie?"

"I wish I knew." It was hard being the subject of rumors, but even more so when his own father was starting them. It was worse because of how badly he wished they were true.

"There's nothing between you?" Miriam wagged a finger at him. "I saw the two of you eyeing each other all through church at my house."

"Then you probably heard what I said about her." Elam tugged at his collar, which suddenly felt too tight. Katie's dignity as she'd walked past his table afterward had impressed him, but the pain in her eyes had been clear.

Miriam tapped a foot. "I hope you apologized and made things right."

"As well as I could."

"So you're in love with her, but—"

"Wait a minute. How did you jump to that conclusion?" Elam lowered his voice so the passengers in nearby buggies didn't hear their conversation when they passed.

Miriam's gloating smile reminded him a lot of his Daed's. "You just proved it by not denying it. Besides, if you made a comment that extreme, you must have been under great duress. The only thing that could make you act so out of character is denying deep feelings." Her eyes bored into him. "Am I right?"

"Sort of."

"It was too bad Katie heard your remark, though." She nibbled her lower lip.

"Yes it was." Elam reached out and patted Miriam's horse, who was snorting and stamping his feet impatiently. "I apologized."

"And you two made up?"

Elam scratched the horse's neck. "There was nothing to make up. Katie said she forgave me for it, so I hope in time she'll forget it. She may already have, since she has a boyfriend who puts her at number one."

"I'm not so sure about that. Jonas seems more interested in cars than Katie," Miriam said with disgust.

"That's a shame," he murmured. "She deserves better."

"I agree." She stabbed a finger in his direction. "You."

Elam shook his head. "She wouldn't be interested in me."

"I think you're wrong about that." Miriam waved Luke over, and they both climbed into their buggy.

With a quick wave, they took off, leaving Elam wondering what his cousin meant by her last remark. Why did Miriam think Katie would be interested in him?

It made him sad to think Katie's boyfriend didn't prioritize her, but maybe he'd outgrow his car obsession the way Elam had outgrown his need to hide his awkwardness behind books. Not that he still didn't love to read, but now he always put people first. Especially one special person.

Katie had groomed her goats well on Saturday, but she and Leah went out to the pen early Monday morning to brush them before Elam arrived. He pulled in as they were finishing. Katie let go of Buttermilk's collar to direct Elam as he backed the buggy with a small trailer attached to it up to the gate. He opened the cage door on the trailer, and Katie let him in the gate.

Buttermilk loved to show off for strangers, so she climbed to the roof of the shelter and refused to come down. Sometimes the best strategy was to ignore her.

"Why don't you take this one to the trailer?" Katie suggested to Elam, pointing to their sweetest, most docile goat. "And I'll take this one."

She picked a feisty one, but both goats came without a fuss, and she gave them each a treat as Elam secured them in the trailer. Then they returned for the other two. The third one balked.

"Maybe if you take Daisy's collar, I can encourage her to walk forward." Katie held a treat in front of the goat.

Before Daisy reached the snack, Buttermilk bounded from the roof to the ground and snatched the treat. Her momentum knocked Katie headfirst against Elam's chest. He let go of Daisy's collar and wrapped his arms around her, stopping her fall. Closing her eyes, Katie drew in a deep breath as Elam's heart drummed rapidly against her cheek. She wished she could stay here forever—warm, safe, and protected. Her dream had come true.

Buttermilk bumped both of them, jolting Katie back to reality. "I-I'm so sorry." She pressed a hand against Elam's shirtfront to push herself away. He seemed as reluctant to let her go as she was to leave the circle of his arms—or was that only wishful thinking?

Elam wanted to go on holding Katie like this, but he released her. When he had a chance, he would sneak Buttermilk an extra treat. That wild goat had given him quite a gift.

When Katie apologized, he struggled to find his voice. "It's all right." His words came out deep and husky. And it was more than all right. He'd thoroughly enjoyed the chance to embrace her.

Buttermilk continued head-bumping them, not hard, but just enough to get their attention. Apparently, she didn't appreciate losing her place as the star of the show. While still steadying Katie with one arm, Elam reached down to nab Buttermilk's collar, but the goat eluded him.

"I told you she was a problem." She sounded out of breath. "I'll try to catch her if you can get Daisy."

He placed a hand on Daisy's collar but stopped to watch Katie chase Buttermilk, who dodged every time Katie got near. After a few quick feints, Katie got a hand on the goat. He couldn't help smiling. She was good at this, and she seemed to love it.

Tugging on Buttermilk's collar, Katie managed to coax the reluctant goat into the trailer. She tossed a few treats through the mesh to keep the animals occupied, while he closed and latched the cage door.

He laughed. "You were right about Buttermilk. She's quite a character."

"Yes, she keeps us hopping." She recounted some of the goat's antics.

He winced at the story of the trampled bread and pies. "All that work gone. At least you can laugh about it now."

"We still haven't made up all that money, but we baked a huge amount the next day, which helped."

Buttermilk kicked at the cage and banged it with her head.

"I'm sorry," Katie said. "I hope that mesh can withstand her battering."

He reached through one of the holes and scratched Buttermilk. "This cage has been through quite a few goats, and we have our share of wild ones, so don't worry."

"I can just picture her breaking through the mesh while you're driving. She'll be happily chomping in the cornfields or gardens where she lands by the time you realize she's gone."

He chuckled. "She'd enjoy that, but I'm not sure about the farmers." Around them, the sky was lightening. "Speaking of farmers, I need to get back to milk the goats. Daed will be wondering what's taking me so long."

She accompanied him to the driver's door of the buggy. He wished she could ride with him so they could continue their conversation, but she'd need to bring her portable storage tank for the milk.

As he got in, Katie said, "I'm grateful your Daed's willing to do the freshening. Maybe becoming a mother will settle Buttermilk. She lost her kid the first time. Have you noticed if your goats get calmer after kidding?"

"Some, but not all. Each one reacts differently to motherhood."

She smiled. "Much the way humans do."

No doubt she would react well. Elam pulled himself up short. How had a discussion of misbehaving goats become thoughts of Katie, marriage, and a family?

Because everything he did lately brought his thoughts back to Katie Kurtz.

16

Katie waited until Elam pulled out of the driveway before hitching up her horse, then she loaded a cooler Leah had packed and started off. He wasn't expecting her until later that morning, but she intended to help him milk the goats. She also hoped to arrive in time to assist with unloading Buttermilk and getting her settled.

When she pulled into the Hertzlers' driveway, Elam was encouraging her goats to move from the cage to the pasture. She parked her wagon behind the barn near the milk shed and hurried over to help.

As soon as he saw her, his eyes seemed to light up. More wishful thinking? "What are you doing here so early?"

"I thought you might need help with Buttermilk."

She hoped Buttermilk would knock into them again, but her curious goat leaped off the trailer, eager to explore her new surroundings. She rocketed into the small outdoor pen sectioned off from the main play yard and headed straight for the climbing tree in the center of the pen.

"It looks like she's going to be happy here," she said. "Maybe she'll want to stay." She understood that feeling.

He smiled. "She's welcome to stay." His expression seemed to add, *and so are you.* But the invitation flashing in his eyes disappeared so rapidly, Katie might have imagined it.

"It's so much fun to watch goats playing." Her joy at being near Elam added extra enthusiasm to her words.

"You really love goats, don't you?" He stepped close enough to almost brush her sleeve, but then edged sideways, putting a larger gap between them.

"Of course. Don't you?"

"Sometimes. Other times they distract me from the work I want to be doing."

"Writing is important to you, isn't it?"

He glanced over his shoulder, as if checking to see if anyone could overhear their conversation, before answering. "I don't know what I'd do if I couldn't write. Ideas spill out all the time, and I'm usually itching to pick up a pen to jot them down."

"Does it bother you to be interrupted?"

"Definitely." He sighed. "When I start writing, it's like I'm immersed in another world, another time and place. Interruptions jolt me out of that place. It's an abrupt shock. Sometimes it can take hours to get back to where I ended."

She'd disturbed him twice the other day. "I'm so sorry I bothered you while you were working."

"And I apologize for growling at you."

"I understand." If she'd lost hours of work, she'd probably be testy too.

He broke their gaze, making her realize she'd been staring at him with admiration. She hoped he hadn't read that in her eyes.

Elam forced himself to look away. "I need to milk the goats so Daed can take care of the freshening." He started toward the barn door. For someone who claimed to dislike talking, he certainly managed to spend a lot of time lately in conversation.

Katie hurried after him. "I'll help."

"You don't have to," he protested. "Mucking out the stalls and helping Daed is plenty. More than enough, in fact."

"I'd enjoy doing the milking."

So would he.

Her bouncy steps brought her close to him. So close, he could reach out and pull her into his arms as he had this morning. He clutched his suspenders and squeezed his eyes shut for a minute to block out those images and prevent himself from acting on his impulse.

Beside him, Katie was still talking, but he barely heard her. Working next to her would be excruciating. "Maybe you could go in and visit Daed while I milk."

"But I like getting to know the goats," she protested. "They'll trust me more if I'm not a stranger."

Elam couldn't argue with that. Nor did he want to. Excruciating or not, he'd enjoy milking with her.

As they moved down the rows, she cleaned the goats as he attached the milking machine. When the container was full, she pushed it into the milk shed and emptied it. He enjoyed her company as well as the help. Milking went much more quickly with them both working.

Ever since Katie had mentioned she was familiar with Emily Fox books, Elam had been curious about her reading. He got up his courage to ask, "So do you read any other authors besides Emily Fox?"

She smiled. "Of course. I read lots of books about the Bible and godly living."

So did he, but he wanted to know about fiction. "That's good. What about novels?"

Her cheeks grew rosy. "We're not really supposed to read worldly novels."

"I know. I'm not supposed to write them either."

"But you do."

He nodded. "I know the bishop doesn't agree, but I try to give my books a spiritual message, so people who read them will have their faith strengthened. I have no way of knowing if I've succeeded, but I pray I have."

"I'm sure your books will help people when they're published."

He debated whether or not he should tell her the truth. He'd better not. That was one secret he could never share.

She went on. "I think that's why I like Emily Fox books so much. They always make me feel closer to God when I read them. You should read the ones you have on your desk. They'll give you some good examples of how to do that."

He let her natter on about Emily Fox and tucked each of her words into the deepest recesses of his heart.

"You asked if I read other novels. I've read a few, but so many of them get their facts wrong. And not all of them strengthen my faith, so I understand why the bishop doesn't want us reading them."

They moved from goat to goat, and Katie still hadn't run out of things to say about her favorite author, but she took time to get to know each goat they milked. She impressed him by how quickly she put even the edgiest goats at ease. She also remembered most of their names. She'd make a wonderful wife for a goat farmer. That thought brought a pang. Would she learn names of engine parts and car models as rapidly? Would she work beside Jonas as he repaired engines? Handing him tools? Cleaning off parts? Teamwork in marriage was important too. He only wished she could continue to work by his side.

"That's the last goat." Elam stood. "Now I just have to clean the equipment. Danke for your help. I finished much sooner than I usually do." He smiled down at her and was pleased when she returned it with a broad grin.

"This was so much fun!"

He laughed. "Maybe the first time you do it." He headed to the sink to wash out the hoses and connectors. "Believe me, it can be a chore on freezing winter days when you have the flu and have to drag yourself out here to work."

"I know. We only have four goats, but sitting in a drafty barn when you're not feeling well is awful. It helps if you have someone else who can do it."

Exactly what he'd been thinking. Well, not quite. He'd been thinking of milking with her. He tried to get his mind back to their conversation. "In an emergency, Daed could do it, but I hate to ask. It's so hard on him."

"I'd be happy to do it if you ever need help."

He wanted to blurt out that he'd enjoy her help every day, but he only responded with, "You're kind to offer. I'll keep that in mind." And he would.

Once the equipment was cleaned and stowed, Elam asked, "Would you like to go into the house to wash up?"

"That would be nice, although I'm probably going to get messy again when I muck out the pens."

"I'd be happy to help you with that."

Katie shook her head. "I'd love that, but you need to do your writing."

His gratitude toward her overflowed. Not only did she not judge him for writing, she even encouraged him. The goats, the writing, her generous heart—was there anything about her he didn't like? Well, maybe her frequent talking. But he was even starting to enjoy that.

Katie and Elam entered the kitchen, and Mose glanced up from the stove, surprise on his face. "Katie, you're early. I didn't hear you drive in."

"I wanted to be sure my goats settled in." She smiled at him. "How are you today, Mose?"

He looked more chipper than usual. "No aches and pains today, thank the good Lord. I prayed I'd have the strength to get all the goats to where they need to go today, and I believe I do have the energy."

"That's wonderful. Oh no!" She pointed to the smoke coming from the egg pan.

Mose snatched it off the stove, but it was too late. The smell of charred eggs filled the room.

"I'm so sorry I distracted you."

"Don't worry," Elam said. "Around here, we only have two types of eggs. Burned or watery."

Mose pretended to glare at him. "Be thankful you have food."

"I am. Besides, my cooking isn't much better, so I'm not complaining."

His Daed shook the spatula playfully in his direction. "*Gut.* Because if you were, you wouldn't get any of these eggs." He sent Katie a sheepish expression. "I don't suppose you'd care to join us for breakfast?"

"I'd be delighted." Not to eat burned eggs, but to sit at the table with the two of them and have the opportunity to gaze across at Elam.

"You don't have to be polite," Mose said. "I know it isn't what you're used to."

"Believe me, when I first learned to cook, I made my share of mistakes. Everyone does."

"Except I've been doing this for three years now, and I've made little improvement." Mose made a face, then took a third plate from the cupboard. He spooned equal portions of eggs onto each.

Katie had already eaten breakfast at home, so she wanted to ask for a smaller portion, but she couldn't risk hurting Mose's feelings. She was grateful for the cooler Leah had packed. At least she could ensure they had a good lunch.

Mose waved a hand to indicate she should sit on the bench across from Elam, who had poured them each a glass of goat milk. Once they'd prayed, she barely lifted her fork to her lips. Yes, she was full and the burned eggs weren't appealing, but those weren't the main reasons. Most of her attention focused on trying to steal peeks at Elam without him or Mose catching her.

"I'm sorry," Mose said, pointing to her plate. "I shouldn't have forced you to eat those. We're used to them by now."

"I was daydreaming. I do that sometimes." She crammed a large bite into her mouth and tried not to choke on the burnt flavor. She washed it down with milk.

"Sounds like Elam. He often sits here lost in thought and doesn't hear me when I talk to him."

Until recently, daydreaming had never been a problem for her, but lately she seemed to be spending more time in her fantasy world than reality. She supposed writers often spent time in their heads while they were plotting stories. She almost said that, but Elam caught her eye, reminding her of her promise. His Daed had no idea about their shared secret.

Mose did, however, notice their eye contact. "If you two are done staring into each other's eyes, we should get the dishes in the sink. We have work to do this morning."

With her cheeks hotter than the burning pan, Katie tore her gaze from Elam's and shoveled in the last of the eggs, following each bite with a gulp of milk. She rose and carried her plate to the sink. "I'll do the dishes."

When Mose and Elam both protested, she said, "You fed me a meal, and it won't take long to wash three plates and glasses." She didn't mention the chore of scrubbing out a burned pan. "I'll be out as soon as I'm done."

"So you'd rather wash dishes than muck out stalls?" Mose had a twinkle in his eyes.

"I'll do both."

She earned a smile of appreciation from him. "You're a good girl, Katie." Then he sent a pointed look at his son, and Elam reddened.

After they walked out the door, Elam may have thought he was out of hearing distance, but his tense whisper floated through the open window. "Please don't do that, Daed. It's embarrassing."

Mose's usual booming voice carried, although they'd gone down the steps. "Nothing wrong with a father wanting his son to be happy. What's embarrassing is a son who's still unmarried and doesn't recognize a good opportunity when he has one."

"Daed, how many times do I have to remind you?" Elam sounded exasperated. "I can't court her."

Their voices faded in the distance, but Katie stood frozen at the sink, his words replaying in her mind. "I can't court her."

Of course he couldn't. She had a boyfriend. Elam would never be so dishonorable as to ask her to give him her heart when he knew it was spoken for.

All the fantasies she'd woven about the two of them crumbled to dust.

Elam's face still burned from his Daed's pointed remarks at breakfast. If Katie hadn't figured it out before, she certainly had now. But why did his Daed persist in throwing them together?

Spending so much time around her, knowing she belonged to another man, was torture. It pained him even more to know Jonas didn't treasure Katie as she deserved. He'd gladly take the man's place if he were offered the opportunity. But that would never happen. If he'd learned anything about Katie, it was that she was loyal and kept her promises. Although at times he wondered if he'd seen flashes of interest in her eyes, he cared about her too much to ask her to go against her principles.

She entered the barn as he and Daed were mucking out the pens. Just seeing her walk through the barn door sent his pulse soaring.

His Daed waved her over. "If you wouldn't mind doing this pen, I'll set things up outside."

She readily accepted the second rake Daed had made Elam buy at the hardware store last night. So this had been his Daed's plan—to leave them alone in the barn together. He hoped it wasn't as obvious to Katie as it was to him. Not that he minded.

As they had earlier, they fell into easy conversation, although this time not about books. Elam marveled he could talk like this to Katie when he struggled to talk to other people. He'd never had such an enjoyable time mucking out pens before.

Their camaraderie made him think about his Daed's plan. What would it be like doing this if she were his wife? They'd spend the morning milking together. They'd have conversations like this. He leaned on his rake, lost in imagining.

"Letting Katie do all the work, eh?" His Daed's voice startled him.

He hadn't been standing there long, had he? Luckily, he sometimes did that when he was planning a book, so Daed might attribute it to his usual daydreaming. No such luck. Daed seemed to be holding back a chuckle. He shook his head.

Elam went back to raking with a vengeance, hoping Daed wouldn't make an embarrassing remark or call Katie's attention to his reverie.

Fortunately, Mose seemed to be feeling merciful that day and simply asked Katie, "Are you ready to help? If my son can keep his mind on the job, he can complete the rest."

"I'll be right out. I just want to finish this pen."

His Daed nodded and left.

She raked carefully, then said in a low voice, "I noticed you seemed to be thinking about something else. Did you need some time to write it down? I can muck out in here after I help your Daed."

Her thoughtfulness touched him. "I appreciate that, but I'll finish this first."

After she left, he could indulge himself in all the dreaming he wanted. As long as he cleaned the pens, of course.

17

When Katie reached the pens, Mose was struggling to direct a frisky buck into a separate enclosure. She hurried over to help.

He looked up. "Did you and my son have a good conversation?"

"Of course." She kept her face and words neutral, but he studied her as if hoping to ferret out a deeper reaction. She wouldn't be surprised to learn Mose had listened in to their conversation, and she was glad she and Elam hadn't discussed writing or books. Or had they? She stopped short as she was entering the gate. *Oh no!* She'd brought it up near the end of the conversation.

The buck wrenched away from Mose, head-butted him, and bolted for the open gate. With a shout, Mose fell and hit his head on the rail behind him. His hat went flying.

Katie rushed to close the gate, but the buck squeezed through, knocking her sideways as he brushed by. The gate hit her in the stomach, knocking the wind out of her. She doubled over and tried to catch her breath.

"What happened?" Elam raced outside. "Daed!" He rushed toward Mose, who lay crumpled on the ground.

"Don't worry about me," Mose said weakly. "Catch the goat."

Elam headed for the gate. "Katie?" He took her arm. "Are you all right?"

The tenderness in his eyes made her dizzy. Breathless, her head reeling, Katie could only point in the direction of the escaping goat. When Elam hesitated, she managed to say, "I'm all right."

"Are you sure?"

Katie nodded. He still held her arm, which was tingling. As much as she didn't want him to let go, she croaked out, "Goat."

Mose bellowed, "Get that buck!"

Elam barreled off, and Katie straightened and dragged in a breath. Her stomach hurt from the collision with the gate, her lungs ached from lack of air, and blood thundered in her ears from the suddenness of the goat escape and from Elam's touch.

Ignoring her pain, she rushed to Mose and kneeled beside him. "Are you injured?"

"Mostly just my pride," Mose admitted. "But I did hit my head and back."

"Should I get a doctor?"

Mose shook his head, then groaned. "Moving my head makes me dizzy. Better keep still." He batted her hand away when she touched his head. "I'll be fine. Just need to catch my breath." He pointed to the open gate. "Shut that, and help Elam. That buck's tricky."

"I'm so sorry." If she hadn't left the gate open, the buck would still be in the enclosure.

"No time for that. Just go."

Katie took off. When she reached the driveway, Elam had grabbed the buck's collar and was marching him toward the pen. She admired his strength and agility as he dodged the buck's horns.

He glanced up and saw her. "You're all right?"

She nodded. "I've been hit by gates before."

"How's Daed? Judging by his yell, he isn't too badly hurt."

"He said he hit his head and back, but he's conscious and talking, so I hope he's all right. He wanted me to help you." She glanced again at the strong muscles that kept the unruly buck under control. "It looks like you have him. I'll go back and tell your Daed."

Katie pivoted and headed toward the enclosure. She'd only gone a few steps when Elam shouted, "Watch out!"

She spun to see the buck headed straight for her, his horns lowered.

Used to Buttermilk's antics, she sidestepped the horns and snagged the buck's collar, but he was much heavier than her does. He dragged her along as he charged toward the cornfield behind the house. Stumbling along, she nearly lost her footing. The buck tossed his head from side to side trying to dislodge her, but she hung on.

Strong arms darted around her, grabbed the collar, and pulled the buck to a halt.

"Danke," she wheezed out. If Elam hadn't stopped the buck, she had no doubt disaster would have followed. But now she was sandwiched between him and the buck's side, and Elam had one arm wrapped around her, holding her close. His heart hammered as fast as hers. His chest was heaving, and they both were gasping for air.

"Katie," he said, so close to her that his breath caressed her ear. "I'm going to move back a little so you can get out."

"I don't want to let go of the collar," she said, but that wasn't her main concern at the moment.

"It'll be all right. I have him." The breath on her ear again made her shiver.

"Are you all right?" he asked.

"I'm just winded." From the chase and his nearness.

He loosened his arm, and, feeling bereft, she slipped away from his warmth and comforting arms. She followed him to the enclosure and hurried ahead of him to open the gate so he could keep both hands on the buck's collar. When the buck was inside and Katie had latched the gate, she and Elam both exhaled loud sighs, but he continued to keep the buck corralled.

"I think I need to put him in a separate pen for now. We can try the freshening tomorrow."

Mose, now sitting up against the fence, weakly said, "Good idea."

Katie went over and stayed beside Mose until Elam returned. He crouched on his Daed's other side. "Do you think you can stand, or would you rather we not move you?"

"I can get up, but I'll need some help."

She and Elam eased him to his feet, and he hobbled along between them. They took the stairs to the porch slowly. One step. Rest. Another step. Rest. Until they made it to the top. He shuffled across the kitchen floor and to his padded chair in the next room. He groaned as they lowered him into the seat.

"Should I fetch the doctor?" Elam asked.

"Neh, neh. I'll be all right."

Katie brought a stool to prop up his feet. "Is there anything else I can get you?"

"A hot water bottle would be nice."

"I'll heat some water and make you some lunch." She bustled out to the kitchen and got to work.

After assuring himself his Daed really would be fine, Elam entered the kitchen. "If you don't need my help, I'll be in the office."

"We'll be fine."

"If anything changes or he needs a doctor, don't hesitate to knock even if I'm typing." He leaned close to her and whispered. "Between you and me, I think he just wants a little attention."

Elam's closeness sent her pulse into double time, but she frowned. He didn't seem very concerned about his Daed. "That was a hard fall."

"I know, but he takes harder falls and gets back up with only a grimace or a groan." When she raised an eyebrow in disbelief, he said, "Trust me on this."

Katie didn't believe him. She was certain Mose wouldn't fake an injury, but after bringing him tea and a hot water bottle, she wasn't so sure. Twice, she caught him smiling. A smile he rapidly changed to a wince. And he used every opportunity to grill her about Elam or to tout Elam's good points as a husband. Even if Mose was exaggerating his injuries, she didn't mind. He could probably use some pampering. But she was beginning to suspect he had an ulterior motive.

She brought in the cooler Leah had packed and fried up bacon for sandwiches. Lettuce and thick, juicy slices of tomatoes from her garden went on top of homemade bread spread thickly with mayonnaise. She completed the plate with a pink pickled egg, homemade pickles, and her sweet potato chips.

She took it in to him, and Mose's eyes opened wide as he took a bite. "Delicious! I haven't had a meal this good since . . ." He swallowed and his eyes grew wet. "You're a wonder, Katie. I sure hope my son sees that."

When she came to collect his plate, he said, "You should take a plate like this out to Elam."

"I don't want to bother him while he's working," Katie protested. His Daed had no idea how troubling it was for Elam to be interrupted.

"Just take it. If you don't, he won't eat all afternoon." He pinned her with a look guaranteed to make her feel guilty. "You don't want him to go hungry, do you?"

"No, but—"

He thrust his empty plate into her hands. "Believe me, he won't want to miss this delicious lunch. He'll thank you for it. I promise."

Maybe after he blasted her for interrupting. But Mose refused to back down. Reluctantly, she descended the steps and headed toward the barn with a fresh plate. When she was far enough inside that he couldn't see her, she stopped and listened.

No clacking was coming from the office. Was he writing notes? Thinking about his next sentence?

They'd had so much fun today. She hated to spoil it by ruining his writing. If only she could set the plate outside the door. But the barn cats that slunk in and out might have a feast.

The room remained silent. Perhaps he was taking a break.

She tapped timidly at the door. "It's Katie. Is it all right to bring you some lunch?"

She heard a chair scraping inside. "Just a minute." Papers rustled, and then the lock clicked open. He eased the door ajar a few inches. "You've brought me a feast! My stomach's been growling since breakfast."

Katie was crestfallen that after all their talk about writing and books, he was still barring her from his office. She craned her neck to see into the office, but saw no paper in the typewriter. "Here," she said, thrusting the plate into his hands. "I know you're busy."

To her surprise, Elam opened the door wide. "Would you like to come in?"

Did he even need to ask?

Hot and sweaty after the chase, Elam had gone into the office, but he couldn't settle down to write. After pacing the floor of the small, stuffy room, he opened the window to cool down, hoping the fresh breeze would invigorate him. Breathing deeply, he tried to get his mind on the chapter he needed to write. Instead, his mind kept straying to Katie and how wunderbar it had felt to hold her in his arms twice that morning.

He forced himself to sit at the desk, hands poised over the typewriter keys, but no inspiration came. Picking up a few of the previous pages, he reread them. It didn't help. He alternated between pacing and pecking on a few keys and pacing again. He'd lost so much time the past few weeks and was so far behind. He had to get something written, but the harder he tried, the more frustrated he became.

When Katie knocked on the door, his heart leaped. She managed to distract him even when she wasn't around. He much preferred when she was. Besides, he hadn't accomplished anything so far.

"Just a minute." He took the page out of the typewriter, turned it and the pages he'd been reading upside down, and hurried to the door.

She stood there holding a plate of food that looked scrumptious, especially when compared to the usual meals he and Daed had. Plus he'd had her lunches before. His mouth watered just thinking about it.

The pain in her eyes made him realize he'd instinctively kept the door closed so nobody could see in. She already knew what was inside—well, not all of it, but he'd hidden that—so there was no reason to block her entrance.

The heartwarming smile she gave him when he opened the door touched him and made him glad he'd let her in. She sat across from him again and watched with bright eyes as he ate with relish. Garden tomatoes rather than store-bought and crispy bacon rather than hardened, charcoaled bits, all on homemade bread.

She laughed. "It isn't necessary to thank me after every bite."

"If you'd tasted what Daed and I have been eating, you'd understand."

"I did have breakfast."

"Believe me, that meal was one of the better ones."

"Oh dear. Maybe I should always bring meals when I come."

"That would be a blessing, but we can't accept. You have enough to do already. Although," he said, leaning forward, "if you'd consider bringing an occasional meal in exchange for a reduced price for milk—"

"Your Daed already offered a reduction for the work I'm doing. I can't take more. You need to make some money."

Elam longed to blurt out his secret. He didn't have to charge her at all, but then if he told her he had plenty of money, she'd realize he'd sold books and want to know what he wrote. No, he couldn't let her know. "I think we can manage to pay for some meals. I'd rather give the money to you instead of wasting it at the grocery store on food we'll only ruin. Edible meals would be well worth whatever price you charge."

Katie quirked an eyebrow. "Actually, if you want to buy your usual groceries, I'd be happy to cook meals for you while I'm here."

"Can we shake on that?" He extended his hand across the desk with a teasing smile. Talk about an ulterior motive. He only wanted the opportunity to touch her soft skin again.

"I'd be happy to." With a lighthearted grin, she reached for his hand.

But when their fingers touched and his hand closed around hers, all joking stopped. Could she feel the electricity shooting through his arm and hand? The warmth and softness of her small hand made him want to hold it forever.

But he had no right to. She had a boyfriend. He yanked his hand back, sending the papers on his desk scattering. They drifted to the floor on both sides of the desk.

He shot up from his chair. "I'll get those."

But he was too late. Katie had bent down and grabbed the sheets. She started to hand them to him, but her hand froze in midair. Her face went ashen.

"What is this?" she demanded.

She pulled the papers closer to her and studied each sheet. Her finger trembled as she pointed to the header at the top of the page. "This says 'Emily Fox.'" She rifled through the papers. "So does this one, and this, and this." She slapped the papers onto his desk.

Elam squeezed his eyes shut. "I can explain." But could he? Maybe it was better just to admit the truth. "The pages say that because I am Emily Fox."

18

"No!" Katie jumped up and fled. She wanted to run and keep running. She'd fallen for a liar.

All those conversations they'd had about books, the questions he'd asked about Emily Fox. He'd said he'd never opened the covers of those books on his desk. How could he have misled her that way? And he'd deceived all his fans. How could she ever trust him again?

She had to get out of here, but she had to at least say goodbye to Mose, even if she never wanted to be around his son again. At least Elam hadn't followed her. She mounted the stairs and stuck her head through the kitchen doorway. Mose had his eyes closed. She didn't want to disturb him if he was napping, but as she eased the kitchen door shut, he sat up.

She waved. "I just came to say goodbye. Do you need anything before I go?"

"A glass of water would be nice."

When she brought him one, he studied her. "Is everything all right? Did something happen with Elam? You didn't have a fight, did you?"

How did she answer that? She'd promised never to tell anyone Elam's secret. "Maybe you should ask your son. I need to go, but I'll be back on Wednesday."

"Katie?" Mose called after her. "Elam might be a bit grumpy when he's disturbed, but he has a good heart."

She nodded to acknowledge she'd heard him, but she questioned his assertion. Did someone with a good heart deceive people? With another quick wave, she shut the door.

All she wanted to do was to leave, but she still had to pump her milk. She crossed the driveway. Still no sign of Elam. She sighed, but whether in relief or sadness, she wasn't sure.

She unlocked the milk shed, hooked up the hose, and turned on the motor. As the milk flowed into the tank, the milk she'd poured in there this morning, a deep sense of loss overwhelmed her.

They'd had so much fun together during the milking. She'd been so happy he'd come out of his shell and started talking to her. But the most important part of his life, he'd kept hidden from her. If she hadn't seen those papers, she might never have known. How could she ever trust him now that she knew about his deception?

Elam sat with his head in his hands. The day had been perfect until a few minutes ago. Then one tiny motion, one brush of his arm had ruined everything. He wished now he'd been completely honest when Katie had seen the Emily Fox books. But if he had, they might not have spent today together. If nothing else, he had those memories.

A motor starting outside his open window meant Katie was pumping milk. She'd have to stay there until the tank emptied. Now would be a good time to talk to her. If she'd listen.

He went around the barn and headed toward her wagon. The minute she noticed him, she tensed. Not a good sign.

"Katie, I don't blame you for not wanting to talk to me. It wasn't fair to keep the truth from you."

"I'm not as concerned about me as I am about all the loyal fans who think Emily Fox is a woman. How could you deceive everyone that way?"

"I'm not trying to deceive people. Many authors take pen names. They write under different names for many reasons."

"But that's dishonest."

"I never thought of it that way," he said. "I make up stories, and no one calls that dishonest. So it never occurred to me that making up a name was deceitful."

She bent to check the milk hose and avoided his eyes. "You let me blather on about Emily Fox books and make a fool of myself? And all the while you were snickering to yourself."

"Not at all. You surprised me when you said you liked the books. I value your judgment, so it was an honor to hear your opinion."

She kept her back to him. "What if I'd criticized them?"

"I would have been glad to hear that too. I always want to do what I can to improve them. I want to keep my readers happy, and honest feedback from them is helpful to me." Elam had to admit, though, hearing praise of his novels, especially from Katie, had been a big encouragement. "I've asked my agent and publisher to pass along the bad reviews. I don't want the positive ones to avoid *Hochmut*. They don't understand why I try to avoid being prideful, but they do it."

Katie looked slightly mollified. "You also gave me the impression you were a struggling goat farmer. You let me believe you were writing your first book, and it hadn't been published yet."

"I'm sorry. I didn't want you to think that, but I had no idea how to tell you the truth. If I did, you would have discovered my Emily Fox connection. I was trying to keep that hidden."

"From me." Her voice was tinged with bitterness.

"Not only you, Katie. From Daed and everyone else in the community. I didn't want anyone to know."

"I can understand that," she said grudgingly.

"I've trusted you with more information than anyone else. That's risky for me. How do I know you won't choose to tell someone?"

Her expression indignant and her body rigid, Katie insisted, "I promised, and I won't go back on my word. No matter what happens, I'd never betray you."

"I believe you. I know you'd never do it on purpose, but if you talk to people, something might slip out."

"And since I talk all the time, you were taking a big chance."

"Well, there is that." He tried to make his response light and teasing, and she rewarded him with a slight smile.

"Jah, I can see it would be better if I never spoke to anyone." Her arched eyebrows indicated she was teasing too.

He took the bait. "Like me." He pretended to sigh. "At least the way I was until someone gave me talking lessons. Now I never shut up."

"That's true." She laughed.

The sound delighted Elam. Did it mean she'd forgiven him? He thought they'd never get back on a friendly footing again. He debated about keeping the friendly bantering going or getting serious. He decided on the latter.

"Katie, I really am sorry I kept the truth from you."

"Me too. I could have told everyone I knew the author Emily Fox."

"You still could." His stomach clenched at the thought.

"I told you I wouldn't. Don't you believe me?"

He looked into her eyes. "I trust you, Katie."

She blushed, but her eyes sparkled. "I know it's hard for you to trust people, especially with private information. With me being talkative, it's even worse. So your trust means a lot to me."

He lost himself in the depths of her gaze. More than anything in the world, he wished he could say the words burning in his heart.

She broke their connection first and ducked her head, her face awash with guilt.

And once again, Elam was reminded she belonged to someone else. He had no right to tell her his feelings. He was grateful when Katie changed the subject back to his books. That was a risky topic, but not nearly as treacherous as his attraction to her.

"Why did you choose to become Emily Fox?" she asked.

"I sent in my first story because it bothered me to see so many books making mistakes about the Amish lifestyle. I wanted to write an authentic story. No one was more surprised than I was when an agent accepted it. But they didn't want me to write under my real name, and neither did I." He was surprised by what a relief it was to finally be able to tell someone about one of the most important parts of his life.

"Why not?"

"I wanted to be anonymous. My agent thought women might not buy a romance with a man's name on the cover."

"There are male authors who write these stories."

She seemed to know a lot about these novels. He wondered how many she'd read. "I know that now, but I didn't then, so I agreed. My agent suggested the name, and the publisher agreed. Given the choice, would you buy a book by Elam Hertzler or Emily Fox?"

"Elam Hertzler."

"Thank you for your loyalty, but not everyone would agree."

"You never gave them the chance. Why not use your real name now?"

"What would happen to Emily Fox? No more books would come out under that name. Don't you think readers would be disappointed?"

"I would," Katie said without hesitation. Then she blushed. "Although now that I know who writes them—"

"You won't read them anymore." He sighed deeply. "I guess I've lost my best fan."

"Maybe not." With an impish grin, Katie added, "That is, if I can find out what the next book is about."

"That's a secret until they release the details."

She pouted. "I should have read the pages I picked up."

"I'm glad you didn't." *Very glad.* She might have recognized herself as the heroine.

"Why?"

"You'll see when the book comes out." Perhaps by then she'd have forgotten some of the details.

She glanced at the hose. "The tank's almost drained."

When she went into the shed, he followed her around as she unscrewed the hose, stowed it back on the wagon, and rinsed out the tank. She even hosed down the floor. Then she said, "I should go."

She sounded as reluctant to leave as he was to let her.

"Katie," he asked as she climbed into the wagon, "will you forgive me for not telling you the whole truth?"

"I already have."

"I'm so glad." Thrilled in fact. "And we can go back to talking again?"

"I'd like that," she said shyly.

So would I.

After being with Elam and the goats, Katie bubbled over with energy. She still wasn't sure how she felt about Emily Fox, but overall, the day had gone well, and she'd been in Elam's arms—twice.

Katie bounced into the house after unhitching the wagon to find Leah browning ground beef and onions. Beside her pan, a pot of noodles boiled. Lizzie was shelling peas.

"It smells so good in here. Yumasetta casserole?" At Leah's nod, Katie asked, "Do you want me to prepare the bread crumbs?"

"That would be helpful." Leah gave her a grateful smile.

"I'll go wash up." Katie returned a few minutes later to crumble the ends of several loaves of bread. She greased the casserole dish while Leah combined the cream soups and sour cream with the other ingredients, then scraped it into the greased dish. Katie sprinkled the crumbs on top, and Lizzie drizzled it with butter.

"You're very cheerful tonight," Lizzie remarked.

"Am I usually not?" Katie teased.

Lizzie laughed. "You're usually in a good mood, but today you're extra cheerful, and you have this . . . glow."

Being in love tended to do that. But Katie couldn't share her secret. Not until she had proof Elam cared for her. His eyes seemed to convey that message, but she wanted to hear words to confirm it. For now, she'd hold her emotions close and keep them a secret.

She'd been so wrapped up in her memories and emotions that she had failed to see Leah staring at her with consternation. But when she did notice her, the wrinkles on her sister's brow meant she had something important to discuss. Leah beckoned for Katie to join her, away from Lizzie's chatter with the boys.

When they reached the far side of the room, Leah whispered, "Katie, I know this is not my business, but I saw something this morning that has me concerned."

Katie could guess, but she waited for Leah to explain. "You and Elam"—her face grew bright red—"were hugging."

"Did you see the accident right before that?"

"Accident? Is everyone okay?"

"Buttermilk knocked me over. I fell and Elam caught me. That's all it was." No it wasn't. To Katie, it had been much, much more than that. Her body still recalled every detail of those heavenly seconds in his arms. The touch of his hands. The solid chest beneath his blue shirt. She closed her eyes and let the sensations wash over her again.

"Katie!"

Leah's sharp call jerked Katie back to the kitchen. Reluctantly, she opened her eyes.

"Are you all right?" Leah examined her face.

Katie hoped her dreamy expression didn't give her away. "Yes, of course." As all right as she could be given the circumstances.

"Well, it looked like the hug lasted longer than Elam helping you after tripping." Leah's skeptical expression made it clear she still had some doubts. "I hope nobody else saw it and misinterpreted it the way I did."

Her sister was never critical, so for her to even confront Katie meant the situation would appear questionable to others. The goat pen was visible from both neighbors' houses, and her family had been home, including Daed. Katie prayed Leah had been the only one to see the embrace. It was a good thing Leah hadn't seen some of the other interactions between her and Elam today.

"Katie, I shouldn't ask this, but what about Jonas?"

Hearing Jonas's name made Katie sick. What had she been thinking? She'd enjoyed Elam holding her. Being around him erased all thoughts of Jonas from her mind. Was she ready to make a commitment to courting, a commitment that led to marriage if she could so easily be distracted from the man she'd promised to wait for?

When she didn't respond, Leah gazed at her sadly. "Is it fair to either man?" She dropped her gaze. "I need to finish making dinner." She hurried over to the counter where Lizzie was removing a stack of plates, but Katie stayed near the window, gazing out into the yard.

It wasn't fair to be falling for someone else when she'd promised to be faithful to Jonas. If he'd felt this way about another girl even a month ago, Katie would have been devastated. Although she had to admit, if he told her now he'd found another girl, she'd be relieved rather than heartbroken.

Even if Elam never returned her affection, Katie's heart had been unfaithful. She owed Jonas more loyalty. She had two choices: cut off her relationship with Elam or break up with Jonas. She wasn't sure she was ready to do either.

19

After Katie left, Elam hummed as he went in to do the afternoon milking. He so enjoyed her company, and he was grateful she'd forgiven him. They could go back to talking and spending time together. Elam's only regret was that he couldn't take the relationship to the next level and ask to court her.

Was his Daed right that her boyfriend had no plans to return to the Amish? His cousin Miriam's last sentence lingered in his mind. What if she was right, and Katie was interested in him? There was only one way to find out. Ask her. The very thought of asking such a question twisted his stomach in knots.

How could he broach the subject? What would he say? He went back and forth with himself until she arrived the next morning, but when she did, he couldn't think of a way to open the conversation.

Once again, she'd come early enough to help with the milking. Instead of falling into their easy banter of the previous time, their conversation moved in fits and starts, Elam's nervousness stopping the flow.

Then Katie shocked him. "I always wondered what happened between you and Rosanna."

Had she read his mind? Had she known he wanted to talk about relationships? She'd given him the perfect opening.

He took a deep breath. As much as he hated talking about that humiliating moment, telling her would give him the opportunity to ask about Jonas.

"It seemed everyone in my circle of friends was courting. I knew it was time to ask someone, so I settled on Rosanna."

"That sounds as if you weren't in love with her."

Elam laughed. "I suppose as a writer, I should be more precise with my words. I had a crush on her, I guess, which passes for love at sixteen."

"I understand what you mean. I had a crush when I was younger. But don't you think those sometimes turn into love?"

"For many couples, yes. And if they marry and know they're committed for a lifetime, they work to stay in love. In my case, it was a childish infatuation, but at the time, it was important to me." Most important, though, was finding a future wife to take his mind off a cute twelve-year-old girl who talked incessantly and followed him around everywhere.

"I'm sorry. I got you off topic." Katie put a hand over her mouth. Her voice muffled, she said, "I promise not to interrupt."

He laughed. "I'll believe that when it happens."

She crossed her arms, but her eyes sparkled. "You don't think I can keep my mouth shut?"

"Well, if you had to ask . . ." He waited for her to empty the container, enjoying her laughter. Then as they started down the next row, he continued his story, "I was painfully shy back then, so even the thought of asking a girl to ride home with me was torture."

"I can imagine," she said, her tone sympathetic.

"Yes, well, the only person I could talk to without stumbling was my friend, Matthew Swarey. I told him I wanted to ask Rosanna to ride with me after the next hymn sing, but I was afraid I'd end up speechless or make a fool of myself."

"Oh, Elam." Katie's soft voice erased some of that long-ago pain the same way she'd erased some of his tongue-tied embarrassment in conversations.

"Anyway, Matthew suggested he'd ask her to see if she'd ride home with me after the singing. He bungled the invitation, and she thought he was asking her to ride with him."

She sucked in a breath.

"When Rosanna gave him such an enthusiastic answer, Matthew realized she was in love with him, and then discovered he felt the same way. I nursed my heartache for years and vowed never to marry."

"She wasn't worth wasting your life over." Her indignant voice made him smile.

"But it's hard because the rejection still stings."

"She was a fool to reject you."

"Actually, she never had a chance, but you wouldn't have done the same?"

"Of course not." A guilty look washed over Katie's face. "At least not back then."

What about now? He had the perfect opening. All he had to do was gather enough courage to ask. He forced himself to say the words, "And what about—"

"Katie," his Daed said behind them. "You're here already?" He shuffled over to them, oblivious that he'd just interrupted a pivotal moment in Elam's life. First Matthew, now his Daed. Was he ever going to get this love thing right beyond the pages of a book?

Throughout the day, Katie had found Elam's behavior confusing. In the morning, he'd been sharing his past, and the conversation had flowed. Then his Daed entered the barn and interrupted them. After that, Elam had become distant and standoffish.

At unguarded moments, she sometimes noticed a look in his eyes—admiration? caring?—but he quickly erased it when he caught her watching. When she'd been in his arms, she'd thought. . . Katie shook her head. Was he fighting his emotions the same way she was wrestling with hers? Or were the feelings she had for him clouding her interpretation of his reactions?

Elam's coldness might be for the best. It would help her to stay faithful to Jonas. But she was unconvinced she was making the right choice. His tale about Rosanna had made her reevaluate her relationship with Jonas. Were her feelings for Jonas similar to Elam's childhood crush on Rosanna? Was it time to move on?

Katie was still unsure by the time she reached home that night. She greeted her sisters, but pleaded a headache. "I'm going to lie down for a bit, but I'll be back down to help with dinner."

"No need," Leah assured her. "It's almost ready." Concern on her face, she added, "You look as if you could use a rest. Take as long as you need."

"Danke." Katie hurried upstairs, shut her door, and stretched out on her bed. She needed to get this settled. She couldn't keep playing this game.

Her feelings for Elam increased the more time she spent with him, but that put Jonas at a disadvantage because they were in a long-distance relationship. If she were seeing Jonas as often as she saw Elam, would it make a difference?

As painful as it would be, she had to be honest with Jonas. She'd had doubts about his last letter that she'd skirted around. She went over to the desk and wrote a letter, agonizing over every word.

Jonas,

For a while now, I've been concerned that you might not be coming back to the church. I pray you do, of course, but with your recent plans, I wonder if we should consider setting each other free from the promise we made three years ago.

Sincerely,

Katie

She slid the letter into an envelope. Rather than feeling relieved, her spirit felt weighed down with guilt. Unsure whether she'd have the courage to send it, she set it on her dresser. She'd think about it over the next few days to be sure she was making the right choice. Then she did something she should have done a long time ago—knelt by her bed and prayed.

Dear Lord, I'm so confused about my relationships with Elam and Jonas. I'm turning my future over to You. Please direct my choices and actions.

Her mood finally lighter than it had been all day, she headed down to help with dinner and the evening soapmaking.

The next day when Katie went to pick up the milk, the letter still lay on her dresser. She agonized over whether to send it, but couldn't bring herself to put it in the mailbox. Could she break her promise to Jonas?

When she arrived at the Hertzlers, Mose greeted her. "Elam will be sorry he missed you. He had to drive to the hardware store to get a part for the milking machine."

She nodded, and Mose looked disappointed. He must have been hoping he could pass along a message.

"Well, I'll get back to work," he said. "Unless you need help."

"I should be fine," Katie told him as she uncoiled the hose. "Thank you for asking."

Mose headed toward the barn, his steps sprightlier than they had been. He'd made an amazing recovery from his injuries from the other day. He'd been lively and active during the freshening, and he seemed to have no back pain today. Elam must have been right.

Elam hadn't returned by the time she finished pumping the milk, so she left feeling depressed. The whole way home, she brooded over whether or not to send the letter. Seeing Elam today might have clarified the issue.

When she arrived home, Leah had set out all the soapmaking equipment. It was nice to have her sisters' help today. The market had moved to fall hours, so they were closed on Thursdays and were open fewer hours on Tuesdays and Fridays. They all worked long hours, but they'd been keeping up with the milk supply. With their own goats still at Mose's for the freshening, that lessened their workload a bit too. And Aaron could pretty much work on his own batches, which gave them extra hands.

Leah smiled at her. "I'm so glad you're here. We're ready to get started." She called out the window to the boys, and they came running in. "Wash up and put on your safety equipment."

"We know." Aaron said.

Katie smiled. Leah was turning into a mother hen. She'd done well at taking over many of Katie's jobs.

Katie was dumping the frozen cubes of goat milk into her bowl when Leah said, "I was putting clean laundry in your room when I noticed the letter on your dresser. I managed to catch the mailman as he was delivering the mail, so it got off safely."

Her sister had sent the letter to Jonas! Cubes of frozen milk cascaded across the counter.

"Katie!" Aaron grabbed the plastic container from her shaking hands. "I think you overfilled your bowl." He picked up the scattered cubes and tossed them into his empty bowl.

At least she hadn't been pouring lye when Leah made her announcement. But what was she going to do now? She'd just broken up with Jonas. Had that been God's answer to prayer?

20

For the next two days, Katie worried about Jonas's reaction when he received her letter. Would he be hurt? Angry? Or would he be too busy training to think about it? How would he respond? She threw herself into the baking and soapmaking so she wouldn't have time to think.

Elam stayed in the office when she arrived to pick up the milk. Sounds of furious typing came from the open window. He must be getting a lot of work done, but it made her wonder if he were deliberately ignoring her. Surely he could hear her wagon rattling past his window. She'd promised not to disturb him when he was typing so she didn't, but she wished she could talk to him, especially because she was so glum.

On Saturday, she drove home and pulled the wagon near the kitchen door.

"Need some help?" Leah called out. She rushed out the door and studied Katie. "You've been looking sad the past few days." Her sister gave her a sympathetic hug. "Is everything all right?"

Katie shrugged. Weighing such huge emotional choices had made her days like a roller coaster. She was worrying if she should have written that letter and how she'd feel if they did break up. And Elam seemed to be avoiding her. She tried to tell herself he was busy with work, but it still stung a bit after they'd had such good talks.

Leah smiled. "Well, maybe it will cheer you to know you got a letter from Jonas. I put the mail up on your dresser."

Already? Could he have answered her so soon? Leah was watching her. "Danke for taking the mail up," Katie said.

"Why don't you go upstairs and read your letter? Perhaps it's good news. I'll have the boys help me freeze the milk."

Katie trudged up the stairs. After being emotionally unbalanced the past few days, the letter had arrived, and she'd know his reaction. But she delayed opening it. After sliding the bills into the drawer, she sat at the desk chair, turning the envelope over in her hands, gathering the courage to read his answer.

Dear Katie,

I'm sorry to hear things are so busy. I miss your letters, but I do appreciate your prayers.

It sounded like he hadn't received her most recent letter. She skimmed it to see, but he made no mention of it. She reread the letter more thoroughly:

I may be coming home to join the church sooner than I anticipated.

She had dreamed of reading those words for years. But why now? Why today, right after she'd sent a letter ending their relationship? Her stomach ached, as did her chest. If Jonas returned to join the church, she'd have to make a choice. Actually, she had to make that choice now before she let herself get too caught up in a relationship with Elam.

She forced herself to continue reading:

Racing school did not go well. I wasn't nearly as good as the others. Turns out everyone else has been racing since they were young children. They started with go-carts and progressed to driving vehicles as young teens. I'm way behind.

When they discovered I'd never been behind the wheel of a car until I was sixteen, they said I had a lot of talent to progress this far. But racing a buggy on country roads doesn't count as experience. It was a hard (and embarrassing) lesson, but I'll stick to repairing motors.

Poor Jonas. To have his dreams destroyed like that. She could easily imagine how crushed he felt now.

I have a week's vacation coming up, so I thought I'd come home, and we can talk about our future.

Love,

Jonas

No! Not now, when she was so uncertain about everything. Would he want to discuss their relationship? Try to change her mind about breaking up with him? Should she reconsider now that he planned to come back to the faith?

Katie wrestled with the questions all weekend, but she was no closer to a solution when she woke on Monday morning. Maybe spending time with Elam would help her decide.

Elam decided the best time to ask Katie about Jonas was when she came to help with the milking. It was easier because they worked side by side, their hands busy, their eyes on the goats. Last week he'd almost succeeded in bringing up the subject before his Daed had interrupted. Today Elam intended to discuss the topic burning in his mind.

But once Katie arrived and they were working together, his hands shook, and he couldn't figure out how to insert the question into their conversation. They worked through row after row, and with only a few more goats to go, Elam got desperate. Katie had once told him to blurt out what was on his mind, so he did.

"How's everything going with Jonas?"

Katie appeared taken aback by his question. He wished he hadn't put her on the spot like that.

"He's coming home, and he plans to join the church."

He couldn't interpret the odd expression on her face, but she didn't seem to be overjoyed at the prospect. Or was he misinterpreting, overlaying his own hopes and dreams on the situation?

"That's unexpected." For Elam too. Deep down, he'd been hoping that Jonas had no plans to return.

"Definitely." Katie kept her head down, so he had only her tone to give him a clue, but she sounded worried and uncertain.

Did that mean things weren't going well? But if Jonas was coming home, they'd work things out. They'd been together for a long time.

Elam needed to step back and get his own feelings for her under control. As much as he wanted to deepen his relationship with her, Jonas had a claim on her heart.

They finished in silence. Then Katie left the barn to talk to his Daed, and Elam retreated to his office. He needed time to come to terms with the situation.

At lunchtime, he was surprised to see Katie in the kitchen, fixing three plates for lunch. Now he'd have to sit across from her and pretend to have an appetite.

But his Daed got her talking about her plans for her soap business. Soon they were involved in an animated discussion about her vision of expanding her business to include goat milk lotions, face wash, lip balm, and other beauty products. She also wanted to make caramel, cheese, and gelato from goat milk.

Elam couldn't pull his gaze away from her glowing face as she shared her dreams. He wished every one of her hopes would come true. He'd do whatever he could to make it a reality for her—and Jonas.

His Daed seemed as enthusiastic as Katie. "You and Elam should form a partnership," he said as he dipped the grilled cheese sandwich she'd prepared into homemade tomato soup.

"I'd like that," Katie agreed with a smile. "I'd be happy to help build up your goat business, if you want."

Daed nodded. "I've been after Elam to do that, but he says this herd size is manageable. What are your thoughts on how the goat farm could be expanded?"

"Well, you'd need an addition to the building and some more pasture for them to graze outside, and why not keep the kids that are born during the next kidding?"

"That's a lot of work," Elam said.

"I'd be happy to help take care of the babies. With the way your

Daed has the freshening set up, doing one-third of the does at a time and spaced four months apart, it'd be easy to increase the herd."

"Easy?" Elam exclaimed.

Katie laughed her beautiful laugh. "I didn't mean there wouldn't be plenty of work. I'm just saying it would be possible."

His Daed homed in on Katie. "Why don't you write a formal proposal and include any other plans you have? I'd like to see you and my son go into partnership on this."

Elam sat there in shock as his Daed expanded on the idea and firmed up plans for the agreement. Then Daed divided up the assignments, making this partnership even more concrete.

Elam liked the idea of doing business with Katie, but if Jonas was returning and planning to join the church, he'd be finished with baptismal classes and they'd be married in two years or so. Where would that leave their partnership? Elam would have a huge goat farm to oversee, and no time to write.

And deep inside, he wished there were a way to make this venture with her more than just a business partnership.

Katie was so excited about the possibilities of partnering with the Hertzlers, she spent hours jotting down ideas on Tuesday. She couldn't wait until tomorrow to present them to Mose, and the less-than-enthusiastic Elam. Besides getting to fulfill some of her longtime dreams, she'd have a chance to work closely with Elam. They already worked well together, and it would be wonderful to spend even more time with him doing what she loved.

All the preparation took her mind off Jonas and the discussion they needed to have. On Wednesday she arrived early to help with the milking, but conversation with Elam was stiff. She wished she knew why he'd gone back into his shell, and why he backed away from her whenever they were near each other.

They'd lost their easy companionship. Something had made him uncomfortable about being around her. If only she knew what had changed, so she could find a way to fix it. But maybe planning for the partnership would bring them together again.

They were cleaning up after the milking when a wagon rattled into the driveway. They both hurried to the barn doorway. A man jumped from his buggy and headed toward them.

Katie's mouth hung open. "Jonas!" She stepped from the barn to greet him. "What are you doing here?" She pressed a hand to her lips, hoping her words didn't sound unwelcome.

"You got my letter saying I was coming, didn't you?"

"Yes, of course, but I didn't know when you planned to arrive."

"I got home late last night," Jonas said. "Your sister Leah told me I'd find you here."

"Yes, I work here two days a week."

Jonas stood, arms crossed, near the opposite side of the driveway from the barn. "I wondered if you'd have time to talk. About our relationship."

Katie glanced at Elam, who stared from her to Jonas and back.

"Take whatever time you need." Elam's voice sounded stiff and unnatural. "In fact, why don't you take the rest of the day off?"

The last thing Katie wanted to do was leave, but discussing her relationship with Jonas here at the Hertzler farm would be awkward.

Although it was the last thing she wanted to do, she said, "Maybe we could take a ride."

Jonas brightened. "I'd like that."

Katie struggled to return his broad smile. Seeing Jonas again made it clear her feelings for him had died. All she wanted to do was go back into the barn with Elam, but she owed Jonas honesty and an explanation.

Jonas reached for her hand as they headed toward his wagon. To avoid his touch, Katie shook the barn dust and bits of straw from her apron. Jonas's expression revealed he'd seen through her ploy.

He waited until they'd climbed into the wagon to speak. "I got your letter the day before I left."

Katie twisted her hands in her lap. "I'm sorry."

"Sorry you sent the letter or sorry you no longer love me?" Jonas's jaw tightened, and he flicked the reins so they could head down the driveway and away from Elam's farm.

Telling Katie to go with Jonas had been one of the hardest things Elam had ever done. He hoped his reluctance hadn't seeped into his words. He'd turned away so he wouldn't have to watch the two of them walking together down the driveway.

As the horse's hooves clattered off, though, he couldn't resist one last peek. They sat side by side in Jonas's courting buggy, facing each other in earnest conversation. Too far away to see their expressions clearly, Elam allowed his writer's imagination to paint a picture of them gazing into each other's eyes, the way he'd often dreamed of gazing into Katie's.

A sharp pain knifed through him. Leaving the pens unmucked, Elam rushed into his office, locked the door, and typed furiously. Words rushed from his heart faster than his fingers could record them. A heart-wrenching breakup in the story mirrored his anguish of losing Katie. Sentence after sentence poured out, flooded with his own distress as visions of Katie and Jonas danced before his eyes.

Once again, he'd made a fool of himself for love. When would he learn that relationships weren't worth this grief?

After what felt like hours, Elam flexed his fingers. He'd written a stack of pages. He only needed to type the conclusion. A happy ending he couldn't envision. Not for his heroine, nor for himself.

The closeness of the courting buggy bothered Katie. Tense and nervous, she edged away from Jonas, wishing for more room on the seat so she could increase the distance between them. When Jonas switched the reins to one hand, she clenched her hands together to prevent him from holding one of them. With a brief look of reproach, Jonas set his hand on his knee.

"I blame myself for this distance between us," he said, "for being away so long, for not writing often enough, for not taking time off to come home."

Each word added to Katie's guilt. "It's not your fault. It's mine." She was the one who'd broken her promise.

Jonas shook his head. "I was so wrapped up in the racing world, I didn't pay enough attention to you. Failing at racing school opened my eyes to what's important. I'll always love cars and engines, but now I want to put God first."

"I can't tell you how happy that makes me, Jonas."

He studied her face. "But not happy enough to marry me after I join the church."

Guilt washed over Katie. She'd made a promise, a promise she should keep. "I did agree to wait, so . . ." She stumbled to stop. Was marrying Jonas God's will? Did God want her to turn her back on temptation, resist her feelings for Elam, and do the honorable thing?

"Forget it." Jonas avoided her gaze, but not before she saw the dampness in his eyes. "I don't want a wife who has to sacrifice to be with me."

Katie wished she could say it wouldn't be a sacrifice, but giving up Elam would be the hardest, most gut-wrenching thing she'd ever done. She pinched her lips together.

His voice husky, Jonas continued, "After I read your letter, I was glad I'd made the decision to come home. I thought"—his voice broke and he swallowed hard—"if I surprised you, you'd reveal your true feelings."

The bitterness in his tone made Katie ache inside. She'd never meant to wound him.

"When I walked up that driveway, you looked shocked and unhappy. So I guess I was right. You did reveal how you truly feel." Jonas's voice was raw with torment.

"I'm sorry," Katie whispered. How could she make up for the misery she'd caused him?

"I'm not. I found out the truth. It just wasn't what I expected."

"I—"

Jonas held up a hand. "I hoped your letter was a mistake, that once you knew I planned to come home and join the church, you'd change your mind."

Katie blinked to hold back the tears threatening to fall. "I wish—"

"I do too. I wish I could go back and do things differently. If only I'd paid more attention to you and our relationship. Instead I was so wrapped up in racing, I lost the best thing I ever had."

Katie stopped herself from reaching out and touching the hand clenched on his knee. She wanted to erase the sadness from his eyes. She wanted to comfort Jonas, but only in the same way she'd want to ease anyone's hurt.

"Tell me, Katie. If I'd come home more often, would we still be together?"

Katie was uncertain of the answer. If she'd been secure in Jonas's love, would she still have been attracted to Elam? The truth rose from deep inside. She'd fallen in love with Elam when she was a young girl and had always loved him. She'd settled for Jonas because she'd been convinced she'd never have Elam's love. Perhaps she never would, but she couldn't commit to Jonas when her heart longed for someone else.

"Never mind. Don't answer that." Jonas closed his eyes and rubbed his forehead. "I saw the way you looked at him."

Had it been that obvious? Did Elam know?

"I won't hold you to our agreement." Jonas turned the wagon around, and his horse trotted back to the Hertzlers'. The two of them sat in silence until he drove up the driveway.

"I'm sorry," Katie said, tears stinging her eyes.

"Me too." Jonas's words came out as tightly as his rigid posture. "I wish you every happiness."

"I wish you the same." Her eyes misty, Katie stared after the buggy until it disappeared.

Elam wished he could ease Katie's pain when she headed to the barn, her eyes filled with tears. They were too far away for Elam to hear what they'd said, but Jonas appeared upset, and so did Katie. Perhaps they'd had a quarrel.

"Want to talk about it?" he asked when she reached the barn doorway.

She gave him a grateful glance, but said, "Maybe in a little while."

As they mucked out the stalls, she worked as efficiently as usual, but her hands shook, and her shoulders remained tense. Her face was paler than usual, and her eyes seemed distant and sad. Elam wished he could reach out and hug her to bring a smile back to her face.

At lunch, she'd almost reverted to the excitement she'd exhibited on Monday, but sadness and strain showed in her face whenever the conversation lagged. Katie and his Daed basically set up the whole partnership without his input.

Maybe that was just as well, because he had too many worries and concerns about the plans. If Katie stayed, he'd be fine with the expansion and other plans. If she didn't, he couldn't handle it on his own.

As their plans grew larger and more grandiose, Elam felt he needed to inject some reality. "I'm as excited about all these plans as both of you are, but I do have a major concern. With Jonas back, Katie likely will be married and starting a family soon. That will leave me to handle all the work alone."

"I have a solution for that," Daed said eagerly.

Elam cut him off. He knew what his Daed's solution would be . . . marrying Katie. He'd love to do that, but—

Katie lowered her eyes, but not before he glimpsed the sparkle of tears. "That won't be a problem. I have no marriage plans. Jonas and I broke up this morning. For good."

Elam motioned his Daed to silence when he opened his mouth. Daed nodded and let Elam take the lead.

"I'm sorry, Katie. That must be painful."

"It was," she said in a choked voice. "I know I did the right thing for both of us, but it isn't easy after all these years. We were promised for a long time."

It took a moment for her words to sink in. Elam had assumed Jonas had ended the relationship, but she'd broken up with him. That put everything in a totally different light. A much brighter light.

"It was one of the hardest things I've ever done, watching Jonas go and not calling him back."

Although he empathized with her loss, Elam was elated that she'd let Jonas leave. Perhaps once she'd healed, she'd be willing to consider another option for her future.

21

Over the next few weeks, Elam and Katie solidified the business plans, but one thing weighed heavily on Elam's mind. He and Katie had gone back to their friendly chatter, and she was becoming part of the family—cooking meals, eating with them, and taking over more responsibilities with the goats.

But the night before they planned to finalize the partnership agreement, Elam agonized all night long. Unless he came out and told Katie how he felt about her, he'd be doomed to working beside her as a business partner and hiding his deepest feelings.

But what if he told her and she rejected him? Then the business partnership would be called off and he'd have no chance to be with her. Could he take that risk?

Too nervous to ask her in person, he penned a letter and taped it to the goat's enclosure outside, so she'd see it when she arrived to help him in the fields. When her wagon pulled in, Elam, tense and anxious, stationed himself just inside the entrance to the goat enclosure so he could see her reaction. If she appeared upset, he'd stay where he was and deal with the fallout later. But if she seemed receptive, he'd head out to join her and ask her again in person.

This was a crazy way to do it, but he was so much better at writing words on paper than he was speaking them, and he wanted to get his words exactly right. His whole future—and hers—depended on it.

As Katie neared the enclosure, his anxiety spiked. She loved to talk, so she'd most likely prefer a verbal request. Why hadn't he thought of that before? With each step she took, the sicker he felt.

He could tell the exact second she spotted the note. She stopped short, then headed toward it. She stretched out a hand, and his heart rate soared. Her fingers had almost reached the paper when Buttermilk, who had rushed over to greet Katie, stretched her head over the rail and snatched it.

Elam burst from his hiding place and rushed into the enclosure to grab the note before Buttermilk ate it. Before he could rescue the paper, Buttermilk gobbled it.

All that planning, all the hours of stressing over just the right words, pouring out his heart onto the page. All of that meaning and his most valuable question now resided inside a goat's stomach.

Perhaps it was better this way. Maybe Buttermilk had just saved him from a painful rejection. Maybe he should keep his feelings to himself. It would definitely be safer.

Katie gave him a piercing look. "Elam, what did that note say?"

He shuffled his feet and muttered, "It doesn't matter."

Tilting her head to one side, she studied him. "If that's true, why did you try so hard to save it?"

What could he say to that? Under her scrutinizing gaze, he opted to confess the truth.

"You know how hard it is for me to engage in conversations." He swallowed hard. "I had something I wanted to tell you, but I was too shy to say the words because I feared they wouldn't come out right, so I wrote them down."

"If you speak the truth that's in your heart, any words will be right."

Although she was correct and, in his heart, Elam knew it was true, he hesitated. Could he face her rejection? For Katie, he'd do anything, even conquer his deepest fears.

But he needed to move beyond the shyness in more than just

words. Taking a deep breath, he reached for her hands—her small, soft hands. Was she trembling too? Then he gazed into her eyes, those mesmerizing green eyes, and spoke what was in his heart.

"Katie, every day I'm around you, I fall more deeply in love with you, so I'm hoping you'll consider adding another layer to our partnership. Would you consider, um—"

She didn't let him finish. "I thought you'd never ask! I hoped and prayed you felt the same way I did, but I couldn't be sure. Some days it seemed as if you cared for me, but other times, you seemed very distant."

"I'm so sorry, Katie. Sometimes I'm distant because I'm thinking about writing, but lately it's been because I was trying to keep my feelings hidden. I thought you were in love with Jonas, so I didn't want to come between you. I felt it wasn't right to have these feelings for you when you belonged to someone else."

"Elam, I wish I'd known. I thought you disliked me or that I'd done something to offend you. I'm glad to know that's not the case. I was so conflicted about my feelings for you. I felt I was breaking my promise to Jonas, but I couldn't stop the attraction I felt for you."

"I wish I'd known too. I worried so much about showing how I felt, but now . . ." He pulled her into his arms. She leaned her head against his chest, and he marveled at how they fit together so perfectly.

She sighed. "When I used to watch you reading in the meadows, I never thought you'd be interested in me."

He was floored. "You were interested in me back then?"

With a laugh, she asked, "Why do you think I talked your ear off? I wanted you to look at me, to notice me."

"You did? All I wished for was that you'd leave me alone." His teasing smile softened his words.

She thrust out a lower lip. "That isn't nice."

"Okay. If I'm being totally honest, I did think you were cute."

"Did you really?"

"Jah, and I still do. Back then, I did wish you'd be quiet sometimes. Now I'm grateful for our conversations."

Katie's cheeks took on an adorable shade of pink. "When we were young, I was trying to get your attention because I had a crush on you."

"I had no idea." He hugged her closer. "It's funny because once I was old enough to be interested in girls, I had a crush on you too."

Her eyes widened. "I thought you only wanted me to leave you alone."

Elam laughed. "I did prefer reading over girls when I was younger, but if I'd been forced to choose, I still would have picked you. Later on, when I developed an interest in girls, you would have been my first choice."

"But you almost asked Rosanna."

"Only because you were too young." He tilted Katie's chin up with a gentle finger so he could gaze into her eyes. "I've been wondering about this ever since you asked me about Rosanna. How did you know about her? I never told anyone, and I'm sure Matthew and Rosanna wouldn't have mentioned it to anyone."

Katie buried her head against his chest, and her words came out muffled. "I asked Miriam to spy on you. One day she overheard you telling Matthew Swarey you wanted to court Rosanna."

"Katie Kurtz, you were *spying* on me?" Elam said in a mock stern voice.

Katie traced his cheek with a gentle finger. "Don't be angry with me. I was young and foolish, and I wanted to know everything about you."

"I'm not angry. I'm . . . stunned." She'd cared so much about him that she had his cousin follow him around. "And I'm a little concerned about what else you overheard." He didn't think he'd said or done anything incriminating, but—

"Nothing bad. Don't worry. And after I knew you were in love with Rosanna, I told Miriam not to listen in again." She lowered her eyes. "I didn't want to hear any more about your feelings for her."

"I wish I'd known you cared about me back then. The fiasco with Rosanna never would have happened."

"I was so sad for you when she started courting Matthew."

That long-ago pain held no sting for him now that he held Katie in his arms. "At the time, I wished I'd never shared my secret with Matthew. But now I'm grateful for his mistake. Otherwise, I wouldn't be here with you."

Katie had been learning that God often replaced losses in life with something even more wonderful. This was perfect proof. He'd kept the two of them for each other.

"But what about Jonas? Miriam told me years ago that you'd promised to wait for him. And you did. I have to admit when she said it, I felt a pang of regret, but I was too shy and too worried about rejection to approach you myself. I almost asked Miriam, but after what happened with Matthew, I was afraid to reveal my feelings again."

"Oh, Elam, I'm so sorry you went through that. And I never would have agreed to court Jonas if I'd known. But once I'd promised to wait for him . . ." She sighed. "It was such a struggle with my conscience to write that letter to him."

"I thought you broke up with him in our driveway."

She couldn't meet Elam's eyes. "I wrote Jonas a letter asking if we should break up, but I couldn't decide whether I should send it. I left the letter on my dresser, and Leah thought she was being helpful, so she mailed it. If she hadn't, I don't know if I'd have ever gotten the courage to send it."

"Then I'm grateful to your sister."

"You should be," she teased. "I was fighting my attraction to you, and then while I was trying to decide what to do, you suddenly started acting so distant."

"I'm sorry I did that to you. I didn't mean to hurt you." His voice held such tenderness it brought tears to her eyes. His love for her shone through every word.

Katie still couldn't believe that after all these years she was here in his arms. In her dream, they'd been together like this, and she'd had her ear pressed against his chest, his heart thumping in her ear, just as it did now. Every detail was the same, except for one: Now it was reality.

She still struggled to believe it was real, but the strength of his arms, the warmth of his chest, the rumble in her ear when he spoke, the tenderness in his voice—none of it would fade away or disappear into mist like dream images.

"I wish we hadn't waited so long to find each other. If only we'd been honest with each other when we were children, we might have been married for years now," he mused.

"We just have to trust that this was God's perfect timing."

"I know you're right, but I can't help wishing we'd figured things out sooner."

"Maybe we needed to learn some things first before we could be a perfect match," Katie suggested.

Elam sighed. "I know what I needed to learn—to get over my fears of speaking to other people and sharing my thoughts honestly."

"Hmm," she said. "Do you suppose God paired me with a quiet man so I'd learn to stop chattering?"

"I've come to like your talking," he confessed. "And I admire the way you speak up about things, but it's good to learn when to be talkative and when to be silent."

"If you really want to keep me quiet, you could do this." Katie reached up and lowered his head down to hers. She pressed her lips to his and lost herself in new sensations, filled with love for this wonderful man God had given her.